David Wheldon was born in Ashby-de-
la-Zouch, Leicestershire, in 1950. He
was educated at Sidcot School and at
Bristol University, where he read
Medicine. He now lives and works in
Bedford. His novel, *The Viaduct*, was
the first winner of the Triple First
Award, instituted in 1982 with the
purpose of encouraging new writing.

Author photograph by M. Kirkup

The Course
of Instruction

David Wheldon

BLACK SWAN

THE COURSE OF INSTRUCTION

A BLACK SWAN BOOK
0 552 99142 2

Originally published in Great Britain by
The Bodley Head Ltd.

PRINTING HISTORY
The Bodley Head edition published 1984
Black Swan edition published 1985

This book is set in 11/12pt Mallard

Black Swan Books are published by
Transworld Publishers Ltd., Century
House, 61–63 Uxbridge Road, Ealing,
London W5 5SA, in Australia by
Transworld Publishers (Aust.) Pty. Ltd., 26
Harley Crescent, Condell Park, NSW 2200,
and in New Zealand by Transworld
Publishers (N.Z.) Ltd., Cnr. Moselle and
Waipareira Avenues, Henderson,
Auckland.

Made and printed in Great Britain by the
Guernsey Press Co. Ltd., Guernsey, Channel Islands.

1

The routine of Alexander's day was planned but the arrival of the letter altered everything. The letter filled him with an unease which was totally disproportionate to its apparent importance. The day, the square on the calendar, had assumed a significance far beyond the ordered routine.

The letter lay at his place on the table of the lodging-house dining room: the envelope was of grey manilla, a deep grey contrasting with the soiled whiteness of the tablecloth. How could he have failed to see the letter at the moment he had entered the room? He picked it up, feeling its peculiar weight. It was not of standard government size but its colour suggested an official origin.

He looked round at the stuffy and over-furnished room. He was alone. He held the envelope in his hands and looked down at it. His name was spelt correctly and the address was correct. The initials of his degree were correct also, a strange fact: he was a graduate of a distant and minor university and his degree was an unusual one.

He opened the letter with a table knife. The thick envelope contained only a single page. He saw, with a certain amount of relief, that the message was brief. He read it rapidly.

The letter informed him that it would be advisable for him to attend a course of instruction. The address was stated. A date and a time were suggested. The letter was obviously official, though the writer's position was not stated. The signature was illegible. The nature of the envisaged course was not even implied: there was an assumption that Alexander would possess prior knowledge of it.

Alexander turned the letter over in his hands. The nature of the stationery surely implied a high authority; this implication was difficult to reconcile with the uncertain meaning of the thing. The message itself appeared to be one of suggestion and not of overt command.

He was re-reading the letter when the landlady entered the dining room. She did not speak; she rarely spoke to her lodgers except on matters of business but she acknowledged the young man's greeting by nodding her head.

'When did this letter arrive?'

'It came by this morning's post,' she said, curious as to the reason for the question. She stared at Alexander. 'Is there anything wrong?'

'No.'

She left the room but she paused in the hall; she saw that he was still standing and reading the letter. She was unable to deduce whether the news was good or bad; she could see only her lodger's uncertainty.

Alexander caught an unexpectedly early bus and so reached his place of work earlier than usual. The university laboratory, a building from the last century, was prominent because of its impressive brick facade which comprised a heavy portico and twenty symmetrical first-floor windows that commanded a view of a cobbled alley and an empty canal. The university was built around such structures as this; buildings complete in themselves but without any composite harmony and which crowded upon one another so that any fineness of perspective was lost. The facade of this building was pretentious – instead of giving onto a ground-floor entrance the mahogany doors were set on the first floor at the summit of a broad-based flight of steep steps. There were no windows on the ground floor, an architect's vagary which gave the place the air of a fortification.

Alexander stood in the hall. The simple action of coming to work had been easy enough; now he found he had no work to do. That is to say he had no work of importance. He stood, uncertainly, in the hall which he had hurried through almost every day for several years but which he had never looked at. He looked at it now, attempting to place his thoughts. One resolution was inescapable: if he were to attend the course of instruction he must seek the permission of the Director.

The Director's secretary looked at him. It was easy to wonder what she had been doing until the knock sounded on her door; there was no work on her desk, only the Director's diary, and she had the bored expression of someone who looks out of a window at an uneventful view.

'He isn't in.' She pulled the desk diary towards her; she ran a finger needlessly down the dates. 'He's lecturing at the Brownian this morning. He should be in after lunch.' She said, as an afterthought: 'I hope he will be; he doesn't always remember to tell me when he has an engagement.'

'I'll come back and see him when he's in.' He had a flitting temptation to pull the letter from his pocket in order to read it again, as the Director might read it. He wondered whether the letter held some slant against him which he could not see, but which a third party might perceive as being compromising or even incriminating. The thought was foolish. It was impossible to read anything like that into the letter. 'Thank you.' He walked back into the hall, closing the door behind him.

Alexander took off his coat and hung it on the back of the laboratory door. He looked down the long narrow room. He glanced at his watch and then at the wall clock. All this was done with a mechanical abstractedness. He put on his white coat.

His colleague had already arrived. He was almost

twenty years older than Alexander. He sat on the wooden laboratory stool, his elbows resting on the bench in front of him; his posture was comfortable. He was a small man, slightly built, and very much a man of habit. 'It's good to see you.' This was his invariable greeting. His speech, always reserved and economical, was occasionally drily humorous. He was an unchanging man, ungoverned by mood. Now, as always, his manner was equable.

Alexander stood behind him. Although he had long since worked amicably with his colleague he found that today he was envious of his narrow powers of concentration.

The older man turned round and adjusted his glasses on the bridge of his nose. He looked at Alexander. 'Is there anything the matter?'

The question was unexpected.

Alexander began to turn away. 'No. I was thinking of something.'

'Is that all?' The older man sounded relieved. 'You were behaving a little strangely.'

'I received a letter this morning.' He tried to sound as though the fact was unimportant. 'It's a vague thing; I don't know what to make of it.'

'Nothing to do with your family?'

'No, nothing like that.' He walked to the door and took the letter from his coat pocket. 'Perhaps you could help me.' He passed the letter to his colleague.'

With his usual methodical care the older man examined the letter-head. He glanced up at Alexander. 'May I read it?'

'Of course; that's why I gave it to you.'

He read and re-read the letter in silence. He turned the sheet over, looked at the blankness of the reverse, and put the paper down on the bench. 'It's vague, as you say, for such an important document.'

This surprised Alexander though there was no reason why it should have done. 'So you think it important.'

'Well, at first glance, yes. I don't know why; the letter

8

lacks any kind of specificity as far as I can see. It's either a piece of administrative stupidity or else it's very aptly written, and with you in mind. It seems to me that you are given the choice of interpreting it in any way you choose. Are you expected to attend this course? Or is that only a suggestion? Perhaps the answer depends on the position of the sender. As that is not at all clear it seems that you are free to interpret the thing, as I say, in any way you wish. But to attend what? What is this course of instruction? How long does it last?'

'I don't know.' Alexander looked down at the bench where the letter rested. 'But you think it important?'

The older man looked at the letter and then at Alexander. 'How should I know? It's so incongruous that you could laugh at it and screw it up. You could snap your fingers at it. Perhaps you would be best off if you did that.' He touched the paper. 'It's fine stationery, if that means anything. Against that, though, the signature is barely legible. Four or five downward strokes, as a man might make who had any number of such letters to sign. What else can you say about it?'

'What do you think they want?'

They were silent for a moment. Then the older man said, 'I can know no more than you.'

'The course starts tomorrow morning. They make that at least clear.'

'You'll certainly need the Director's permission.'

Alexander bent down and picked up the letter. 'Why did they ask me? How am I known to them? I only moved into my present lodgings a week ago: how did they find my address?'

The older man shrugged his shoulders. 'You, of all people, must know.'

'I can think of no reason for such a letter.'

When his colleague spoke again it was with more animation than was usual with him. 'I can tell you this, Alexander. You seem concerned about this vague letter; more concerned than I would have thought reasonable. I've never seen you like this before; you've always been the one to ignore anything irrational. You've always seemed to take life very much as it comes. Of course this letter is official, but in the past you've laughed off all the official vagaries with the rest of us. So why does this letter have you worried? It's a piece of paper. It states nothing clearly. It isn't a summons, let alone a reprimand. If it's the vagueness which concerns you, there are a dozen explanations for that. Perhaps the official who dictated the letter did so after a hard stint of lunchtime drinking – you know how some of them drink at lunchtime – or perhaps the typist had tried to cover a mistake in dictation.' He stopped talking, suddenly.

'There seems to be something purposeful about the vagueness.'

'How can you tell that?'

'It's somehow relevant; I don't know what to think.' He smiled as though at himself. 'I don't know what to do about it.'

'You could get the Director's permission and go. That'll put your mind at rest; the letter's point will at least become clear.' He turned back to the bench. 'I must get on.' He paused, though, in thought. 'The Director will give you permission. I know that,' he said.

'How do you know that?'

'He will have no more idea than I do about the letter's origins. He'll give you his permission; he hasn't got where he is now by contradicting men who might possibly be more important than himself.'

Alexander walked back to his own bench. The letter was folded in his pocket. He stood in silence before the window. The day had significantly altered. He looked down at his bench and saw the open work-books with his own writing, in confident black ink, traversing the pages. For some reason there seemed to be a futility about them. His work was suddenly unsatisfactory.

He found the air in the narrow room vitiated and oppressive. He looked across at his silent colleague who was now engrossed in the compilation of a table of figures; he felt envious of his focussed concentration,

10

but he did not know quite why.

He left the room and walked down the corridor, stopping at a terminal door which led to a room so narrow that it might once have been a blind continuation of the passage; he opened the door of a glazed book-case which the Director euphemistically referred to as the departmental library. He took out a government gazetteer and looked, without any particular hope, for the town where the course was to be held. He found it; this surprised him. The town was well over a hundred miles away but it appeared to be on a railway. He examined the small print and found a statement of the population. The place was not so much a town as a large village. Various other facts were given. The parish church was dedicated to a king rather than to a saint; Wednesday was the early-closing day. The gazetteer was an old edition and the various written statistics must now be inaccurate. He returned the book to the case and closed the door.

The examination of the book had been the first objective thing he had done all morning. He suddenly felt tired, as though he had not slept well the previous night. His thoughts wandered; he wondered what he would be doing now had not the letter arrived: he realized that he had begun to deceive himself that, in a sense, he had been expecting it. He could not concentrate. He went back to his room.

Sitting in the one comfortable chair in the laboratory he asked himself the question: why had he put so much emphasis upon the importance of the arrival of the letter? Was there something – one apposite phrase perhaps – which spoke above the diffuseness and the vagueness of the typewritten fact? There was no doubt that he had read more into it than its typed words warranted: had the time of its arrival been of some significance?

He again left the room and walked up the corridor to the hall; he had a suspicion that his own lack of ease was making his colleague irritable.

He was standing in the hall when the front door opened and the Director entered. The Director, a fat, sedentary man, was out of breath and sweaty about the face; he had obviously just run up the steps of the building. He was too preoccupied to acknowledge Alexander; he made his way to his own office and began talking, without pause, his flat voice breathless.

Alexander followed him in.

'Two slides missing.' The Director gasped after speaking the words. 'I'm going to be late.'

The secretary was searching through the slide-folders.

'I don't want a reputation for lateness. It does the department no good at all.'

Alexander interrupted him. 'Would you mind looking at this letter for a minute?'

The Director made a pretence of not having heard him. 'Both slides are important; particularly the one with the cumulative percentages.'

Alexander knew these two slides; they had been through so many projectors that they had become scratched and blanched and somehow redolent of the Director's attitude towards what he called research. He held out the paper. 'It will only take you a minute to read this.' He found that he had spoken rather sharply.

The Director looked at him for a second, arrested in his pacing of the room. He was about to say something, but he took the letter. He lowered his gaze to the paper. He read the letter in perhaps thirty seconds. He gave it back to Alexander. 'Do you want to go?' He seemed as perplexed by Alexander's manner as by the letter.

'I think I have to go.'

He was interrupted by the Director's exclamation at the secretary's finding of the more important of the two slides. He held the slide up to the light of the window to check its identity, oblivious to its scratched fadedness; he put it in his breast pocket. He walked towards the door, rubbing his pale hands together.

In the hall he turned back to Alexander. 'It seems to leave it up to you,' he said.

12

'Do you think the course would benefit me?'

'I don't know. Possibly it might.'

'May I have your permission to go?'

'Yes. You have my permission, for what it's worth. It doesn't seem to be in my hands.'

Alexander held the front door open for the Director. 'Do you know anything about this course, Sir?'

The Director was looking downwards, searching the street for his taxi. 'No,' he said. 'I know nothing about it.' He began to walk down the steep steps, slightly crab-fashion, half sideways, as though one leg were shorter or weaker than the other.

The older man did not turn from his work. 'I saw the Director go,' he said. He put an ironical emphasis on the word 'Director'. 'You had no trouble getting his permission?'

'None.'

'That's in character.' His expression did not change; he was absorbed in his work and he spoke obliquely. 'He always manages to make you aware of it when he's invited to lecture at the Brownian. It's only a room.' Sarcasm was implicit; an invitation to speak at the Brownian Institute was something of a mark of success. 'He'll have a good audience. I would be there if I hadn't heard it before.' He put down his pen. He had, perhaps, reached a break in what he was doing; he turned to look at Alexander. 'What are you going to do about this letter? You obviously feel it to be important.'

Alexander was not irritated by the fact that they had travelled over this ground. At the same time he knew that further discussion of the letter would get him nowhere; there was very little more to say. 'Perhaps it's important only because I sense it to be so.'

'No. I know you better than you think. You aren't act-ing on instinct. Yes, the letter is vague. It's almost mean-ingless to me. It's perplexing, perhaps, but not worth more than a moment's thought. That is, unless you have seen some direct significance which escaped me.'

13

'I'm not sure about that; if it's so I can't communicate it.'

The older man looked at Alexander in bewilderment. 'What do you mean? You have been showing your reaction to that letter by everything you've done this morning. You certainly have been acting oddly; you've been reacting very strangely to something that surely hardly warrants a moment's thought. You've been irritatingly indecisive. You grasped at my suggestion that the Director's permission or veto would be required. You even seemed to wish to pass onto the Director the final decision. It's all out of character; very much so. What has happened? Is this the first letter?'

'It's the first letter; the only letter.' He paused; he had nothing to say; had he spoken further it would only have been out of deference to a man he had known for many years.

'Perhaps . . .' The older man looked at his watch. 'The morning's all but gone. We could discuss this over a drink in town. You need to get this out of your system; it's doing you no good.'

'No, I must go and find the time of the train.'

The older man still looked at him. 'Use my phone.'

Alexander was already taking off his laboratory coat. He threw it over his stool and walked towards the door. He put on his overcoat. 'I'll walk down to the station.' He looked round the room briefly. 'I need to get out for an hour.'

A disruption of the train services and the lack of information had stirred up the travellers in the booking-hall. The timetables were cross-hatched by scorings in blue pencil and the alterations and cancellations were difficult to read and unclear when deciphered. Behind the embrasured ticket windows the two clerks referred the questioners back to the timetables. Alexander had been standing at one of the windows for some time. He had felt the need to keep the identity of his destination secret from the growing queue behind him. He looked in at the window; behind the smeared glass the clerk's face was unclear and he looked unwell, an impression strengthened by the greenish miasma imparted by the high gaslights.

He stood at a platform's edge. In the past he had travelled from this terminus innumerable times. Now, even as mundane a thing as catching a train had assumed an irrational complexity. For some reason it was difficult to separate the important from the unimportant. He thought back to his wakening in the early hours of the morning, before he had known of the arrival of the letter. Even as recently as that he had never known how precarious and ignorant a state of mind self-confidence was.

The connections were long behind him. It was early morning by the time he reached the small town in which the course of instruction was to be held. The train stopped as it had stopped a dozen times before. Only the sign-board on the side of the station building was different. The lamps were still lit but their light was pale and unnecessary.

He left the station and walked through the early-morning town to reach the place where the course was to be held. He remembered the location of the road from the map in the gazetteer. The road was wide and the houses were large and well separated; they had the look of nineteenth-century villas, each imposing but all built to the same design. They followed the contour of the hill, along the road which traced its way across what had been steeply rising moorland. Above and behind the houses the hill steepened to a south-facing scarp where gorse and bracken grew between the rocks. Higher still the ridge of the hill was indented against the sky and blank rock terraces were enshrouded by the haze of distance. He lowered his gaze and stared at the stone houses and their very private walled grounds.

It was not easy to decide which of these houses was the one specified in the letter. Any one of them would have been an unusual place to hold a government

15

course. The gate-posts were not numbered and the names of the houses, carved on stone copings by the gates, were typical of their age. He looked at the letter again though he knew the number of the house from memory: twenty-eight. He glanced down the street. At first he thought that it might be possible to identify the house by counting the buildings from the beginning of the road. He saw very quickly that this was not possible. Down at the bottom of the hill (where the numbering of the houses presumably began) there was a row of cottages which had been allowed to become derelict. Time had so destroyed this terrace that the individual cottages, roofless and half hidden by bramble, could not with certainty be distinguished.

He walked back up the road to its termination at the moor's edge, examining the houses as he walked. One house was different, though it was not at first easy to tell what set it aside from the rest. He had stood at the gate for some time before he recognized the mark which had made him pause. The tall gothic facade, heavily elegant, had been spoiled by a black iron fire-escape which, descending in a series of zig-zags, had been constructed without any regard for the appearance of the building. The bolts which supported the escape against the wall had rusted and red streaks tearfully stained the stonework.

Alexander walked to the gatepost, a tall stone structure which held heavy hinge-irons but no gate. The words 'Brackenhill House' were carved in the stonework. He looked at the house and saw the blank uncurtained windows which stared dirtily between the metal steps and the bolted rails of the fire-escape. To the right of the drive was a lodge cottage; the door of this was open and he peered in. The tiny room inside was dark and littered with dead leaves and the air smelled of dry rot. The stairs at the far end of the room were uncomfortably steep and the windows were small and few. The lodge had obviously been built for its rustic outside appearance rather than for the comfort of the long-vanished lodge-keeper's family.

He walked up the drive, a direct tar-macadamed road

across what had once been a formal garden. Beneath the pillared porch he paused in front of the door of the house. To the right of the door, upon a pilaster and at eye height, the two numerals 28 were painted.

It had gone ten o'clock. The hour had sounded from a church tower which rose above a clump of trees across the valley. The tower had a disproportionately large clock-face, the hands and numerals of which had the appearance of being recently re-gilded. The sun caught the gilt hands and made the hour they pointed to an hour of unusual significance. Perhaps this was due to the size of the clock-face or to the prominent gilding: whatever the cause, the angle of the hands (they pointed to three minutes past the hour) held some peculiar and direct importance.

Alexander had already knocked at the door; this had produced very little sound. No bell-pull had been visible. He was about to knock again when the door was opened. It was clear that it had not opened for him. A man in a black suit walked out of the house and down the two steps from the door without looking either at the servant who had let him out or at Alexander. The door was closed behind him. He stood quietly, doing nothing more than to look out across the valley, apparently pleased by the sunlit view of the edge of the town and the silver river and the green water-meadows. He stood there for some time, indolently. He had run down the steps as though in a hurry to get out of the house; now he had lost any sense of hurry.

He was dressed in the manner of a public servant but his suit was well tailored. He was not tall, though his leanness emphasized his height. He had straight and very coarse black hair which contrasted with the pallor of his face. In one of his hands he carried a book. There was something about the way he carried it – some unconscious gesture in the manner in which he gripped it – which suggested that he did not value this book at all; that it had, perhaps, been thrust into his hand on his leaving the house; that his acceptance of it had been an act of politeness. The book was covered by a dust-jacket of a sultry red colour. The title, *Identity, Communication and Significance* was printed boldly on the spine.

The official (Alexander could think of him only as an official) turned from his examination of the valley. He looked at Alexander and seeing that Alexander had noticed the title of the book he smiled.

'I'm sorry for being intrusive.' said Alexander.

The official looked down at the book, balancing it on the palm of his left hand as though judging its weight. Then, unexpectedly, he tossed it to Alexander. He began to walk away from the house; he did not even wait to see whether Alexander had caught the book. He put his hands into his pockets and jingled keys and money. As he walked he looked up at the broad sky, and, smiling, he looked briefly up at the sun. The tower clock tolled the quarter.

Alexander, aware of his lateness, knocked at the closed door again, and receiving no reply, he searched in the bank of ivy which grew against the wall for a bell. He found the bell-pull, an unpolished knob of brass set in a cup of the same metal green with verdigris. As he pulled the knob he heard the scraping of the wires behind the door-jamb.

The door was opened by a man in an apron of unbleached cloth.

'My name is Alexander. I'm expected here.'

The man who had opened the door scratched his head, puzzled. He looked again at Alexander. 'Yes?'

'I was summoned here to attend a course of instruction.'

The man in the apron shifted his stance. As though he did not know what to say he glanced down the drive, pretending to be attracted by an imaginary event down by the lodge gate. A female voice sounded behind him; he was pushed aside. 'Take no notice of him, Mr Mause. He isn't really allowed to answer the door anyway.' The woman saw Alexander clearly for the first time and

18

realized her mistake. 'Oh. I thought you were Mr Mause coming back for something. It was difficult to see you properly with the light behind you. You're slightly similar.'

'Was Mr Mause the official who has just left?'

'Yes, but he's a doctor.' She looked at the book which Alexander carried. 'Did he give you that?'

'In a sense. He threw it to me as he left.'

The woman pulled a few strands of hair from her face and smiled. The smile changed her appearance. Her smile was pleasantly perceptive and suddenly gave her the air of possessing a great depth of hidden kindliness. 'That's just in character; exactly what you'd expect him to do,' she said. 'The book was one of the master's; he's been trying to give copies of it to Mr Mause all morning. Mr Mause kept on leaving them all over the house when he thought the master wasn't looking. He was going to leave that one on the hall table when he was leaving, but he caught my eye and decided he'd better take it.' She walked slowly down the steps, past the man in the apron. She stood underneath the porch near Alexander, rather in the way Mr Mause had done. She was obviously pleased to be out of the house. 'Have you been here long?' Her manner was conversational.

'No, I have only arrived a few minutes ago. I don't know this town at all.'

'Did you come by train?'

'Yes. I walked up from the station.'

'Then you won't have seen the town properly. It's an interesting town; we get a lot of visitors. Did you see the church?'

'No, I've only walked through the town.'

'The church is something you ought to see. It's kept locked now, but the chemist across the square keeps the key for visitors . . .'

Alexander looked past the talking woman and beyond the man in the apron and saw the dim hall of the house. The interior, thus seen, was somehow unexpected. The walls were painted cream and the inner doors a dark

19

chocolate brown. The paint was highly glossed and reflected an uneven light from an unseen window. A staircase without a carpet rose distantly to an invisible window. Flowing through the hall and out of the front door was a cold and steady draught which bore the slight but distinct smell of phenol; this smell reminded him of a hospital he had visited in his childhood.

'. . . I do my share in church,' the woman was saying. 'I've got my set days on the cleaning rota.' She appeared to be tired of standing outside; she turned to Alexander. 'How long will you be staying here?'

'That is one of the first things I must find out.'

She nodded her head briskly. The man, still ignored, made his way heavily back into the interior of the house.

'Well . . .' She paused. 'Why did you say you were here?'

'To attend a course of instruction.'

'Where are they holding that?'

Alexander felt himself overtaken by the familiar exasperation which had never been far from him since the arrival of the letter. The letter itself seemed to be of far less importance than it had been in the city; anyway, he had memorized it. 'It's to be held here.'

'Is it?' The question was politely asked. 'Are you sure of that?'

'I think I am.'

'Are you sure you have the correct address? Don't misunderstand me; it's a large house and I don't know everything that takes place.'

'This is the address I was given.'

'Well, it must be so. It is, as I say, a large house . . .' She paused. 'I'm Mrs Killinger.'

'I see.'

'Well, I thought I ought to mention my name to you so that when I go back in and find out about your appointment you'll be able to mention it if anyone asks you. Otherwise it would seem odd, just waiting outside a house door without any particular reason.

'You should really have stayed down by the lodge gate

and not come into the premises at all; as it is, if anyone asks you what you are doing here, you'll be able to say that Mrs Killinger is attending to you.'

'That all seems unnecessary.'

Mrs Killinger's expression showed that she concurred with this. 'I quite agree with you,' she said. 'Nevertheless, if you remain here, I'll go inside and see about your appointment.' She walked back up the steps and into the house, closing the door behind her.

Alexander's exasperation returned with a new intensity. The clock in the valley tolled the half hour. He waited in angry silence, looking at the book in his hands. The title might have interested him under different circumstances; now he was aware of his lateness. He opened the book and noticed that the pages were uncut. Why were they uncut? No modern book had uncut pages. Why had Mr Mause been so uninterested in this book that he had given it to – indeed, thrown it to – the nearest stranger? And why was Mr Mause addressed as 'Mister' if he were, as Mrs Killinger had said, a doctor?

The door opened. Mrs. Killinger stood at the threshold. 'We can find no record of your having an appointment.'

'You must! It was clearly stated!'

Mrs Killinger seemed uncertain. 'What did you say your name was?'

'Alexander.'

'What time was your appointment?'

'It was for nine.'

'Nine! That's some time ago: you should have said that before. I had no idea that you were so late when I came out and stood talking to you.' She stopped talking; her air of uncertainty had increased. She tapped her upper teeth with a thumb-nail. 'Nine.' She turned and glanced back into the house. 'That might explain it, though it isn't my province. Different staff are on duty until nine-thirty; they have their own appointments book which I have never seen; I don't know where they keep it.

Mr Gaughlin's in charge of the staff who are on duty for that shift.'

'What should I do?'

Mrs Killinger said nothing for a moment. Then she said, 'You might as well come in.' She shrugged her shoulders as though she had waived a cumbersome, but usually inflexible, rule.

He was led quickly through the hall, Mrs Killinger walking very rapidly, the hard soles of her shoes noisy on the linoleum. 'If you put your case there,' she said, pointing to an alcove near the stairs where a telephone stood on a varnished desk. She did not linger there; she opened a further door which gave onto a dark and high passage. At the end of the passage was a kitchen lit by slanting skylights. A range was set against the wall opposite the door; several saucepans were boiling. The air was steamy; the painted walls were wet with condensation and heavy drops fell periodically from the glass of the skylights. The room was suffused with a vaporous and spicy smell.

They both stood in the room. Mrs Killinger seemed uncertain as to what she might do next. 'I'll introduce you to Mr Apsleigh.' She paused as if wondering where he might be found. As she thought, she spoke. 'He looks after the complete appointments system. He should know about your arrival. If I can't find him then we'll have to send someone down to Mr Gaughlin's house.' She looked round the room as though she were unfamiliar with it; an unexpected action; she must have known, or might have been expected to know, the internal structure of the house very well. 'The first thing for me to do is to find Mr Apsleigh.' As though she had made a decision that was to her satisfaction she left the room.

Alexander began to pace the room slowly. The intense smell of the food that boiled on the stove permeated the air. He was aware that it was also permeating his own clothes, and the fact had begun to distress him for he knew that the smell would cling to him. Besides, the heat of the room was almost intolerable; the stove must have been stoked with unnecessary vigour earlier in the morning. The steamy atmosphere of the room was saturated with moisture. Alexander stood in the centre of the room. It was relatively quiet. Apart from the muffled rolling sound of the boiling pans and apart from the splash of the drops of condensing water falling from the glass of the skylights there was a creaking from the further woodwork; it seemed as if a flight of stairs lay behind the match-boarding, a well-used flight of stairs up and down which people were incessantly walking and continually passing each other.

Despite the circumstances in which he had first met her he had liked Mrs Killinger. Her angularity had had something comfortable about it, and she had been genuine in her kindliness and in the trouble she had taken in her attempt to set the young man at his ease.

He heard the sound of voices in the passageway outside the room.

'Well, where is he?' The voice was wheezy and asthmatic and gave the hearer the impression that it had spoken through layers of linen.

'I took him into the kitchen.' This was recognizable as Mrs Killinger's voice, but it was so indifferent and flat that Alexander had difficulty in assigning it to the woman. 'I suppose we must send out to Mr Gaughlin.'

'I suppose we must.' There was a muffled irony to the wheezing voice. 'Tell Robert to cut down there immediately.' It paused. 'Wait: tell me again his name, the time of his appointment and the length of time he has been kept waiting here.'

Alexander did not catch the muttered reply to this. He had, obscurely, the impression that the things he had overheard had been intended to be overheard.

'The kitchen!' exclaimed the muffled voice with emphasis. 'What a place to have put someone you don't know! How important is he?'

'I don't know.'

'You ought to have shown him to the waiting room at

23

the front. Did he look like an official? You ought to have taken him to the waiting room at least. I know it's difficult to think of these things on the spur of the moment, but one has to.'

'It was difficult enough to know what to do without validation from Mr Gaughlin's books; I didn't know what I should do; this doesn't happen very often and one never knows what to do.'

'That's beside the point now. How long has he been kept waiting? Long?'

'Not very long.'

'You are right. It's an impasse. One never knows what to do when these things occur.' The muffled voice was dubious and hesitant.

Alexander found the sensation of being talked about as a cipher, an unknown quantity, a person of indeterminate importance, so unusual that he walked to the door and looked out into the dark passage. The man and the woman stopped talking immediately and stared at each other. Alexander looked at the man. 'You must be Mr Apsleigh.'

'No, I'm not.' The asthmatic man did not look like a servant though his mannerisms were those of one. He was dressed like a country gentleman in brown tweeds. He wore knee-breeches and heavy walking brogues. His face would have been naturally florid but he was sweating as though he had just been taking, or been interrupted in, heavy and unaccustomed manual exercise. He looked as though he had been flattered by Alexander's remark. 'I'm his assistant,' he said. His thick, slow voice contrasted with the outdoor appearance of his dress; the flattered expression seemed to be no more than silly unless it was to be taken in a context which Alexander did not fully understand. He twitched at his coat, not out of nervousness but rather in the manner of a man preparing himself for some encounter. His whole attitude was, apart from a deference he thought due to Alexander's inference, that of a man interrupted in some sporting event but behaving politely until circumstances permitted him to return to it.

The three of them stood in the hall. Alexander felt the initiative to be his; his earlier uncertainty had gone. 'Well? I would have been here at my appointed time had things not conspired against me.'

The man, speaking quickly, made it difficult for his hearers to distinguish his words from the pulmonary wheezing. 'Your appointment has still to be ratified, sir.' His face was distinctly cyanosed. 'I'll get Robert to go down to Mr Gaughlin's house. That'll be the best thing to do.'

'Is it far?'

'Five miles perhaps.' Mrs Killinger spoke; she gestured to the gasping man, indicating him to be quiet.

'That seems a long way! Why should this Robert travel five miles on my behalf?'

'Oh, sir, you mustn't worry about that. After all, you say that you have an appointment.'

'I have a letter, certainly.'

'That isn't the same thing as having an appointment, but we'll have to let that pass. Robert must go; he'll have to, if we can find him.' She turned to the assistant. 'He could borrow Mr Apsleigh's bicycle.'

'It still seems a long way.' Alexander looked from Mrs Killinger to the man. 'He won't mind?'

'He won't have to mind if I tell him.' There was something rather powerless in the way in which this remark was delivered. 'It's all downhill.'

'And, of course,' said Alexander, grinning, 'if it's downhill all the way to this Mr Gaughlin's house, it must be an uphill journey all the way back.'

'That hardly matters,' said the asthmatic man. 'It's not much of a hill if the truth be known, and Robert is a fit young man. Besides, Mr Gaughlin will be almost certain to give him something to drink when he gets there.' He turned to Mrs Killinger. 'Do you know where Robert is?' His voice was low and secretive.

'Not at the moment, no. I'll try to find him.'

Robert was easily found. He was a tall, well-built

young man with an inexpressive face and thick, fair hair. He was dressed in a faded blue shirt which lacked most of its buttons, showing his strong chest and flat abdomen. His face was flushed as though he, like the other man, had undergone or been interrupted in some kind of physical exertion. Perhaps he had been running. He recovered his breath rapidly, in the manner of an athlete.

'Robert, you're to take Mr Apsleigh's cycle and go to Mr Gaughlin's. Ask Mr Gaughlin – or any of his staff – if they have any knowledge of an appointment for this man: his name is Alexander.' Mr Apsleigh's assistant delivered these words in a slow and breathless monotone.

Alexander was alone in the hall with Robert. The two older people, as though relieved at discharging their responsibilities so easily, had immediately walked away in the direction of the kitchen when the order had been given. From the open door of the kitchen, seen down the dark corridor, a thin drifting of steam emerged.

Alexander was uncomfortable in the presence of this youth, Robert.

'What goes on in this house?' Alexander had been constrained to speak because Robert's stare, speculative and calculated, had grown unbearable.

Robert, as though set in motion by this question, turned his head on his muscular neck and stared out of the open door. 'Varies.'

'What do you mean?'

'Varies on who comes here.'

'How can it vary with those who come here? Do you mean the visitors?'

'Yes; that kind of thing. What goes on here varies with the visitors.' He seemed to be pleased at his own enigmatic reply.

'How long have you been here?' asked Alexander.

'A year. I suppose a year.'

'Do you like it here?'

Robert smiled as though he found the question both

26

pointless and inept; he still stared out of the open door. It was impossible to know what he was thinking. 'You could say I liked it here.'

'What is the nature of your appointment here?'

Robert had had enough of this. 'You must be important if they want me to go out for you on Apsleigh's cycle. The thing hasn't been used all winter; tyres will be flat.' He leaned back against the wall, powerfully inert; he shifted his stare back to Alexander. 'I take it you don't know how long you'll be here.'

'I must find that out as soon as possible.'

Robert nodded his head slowly. 'I shouldn't worry about that for the moment. You could have a good time here if you go about it the right way.'

'It's good of you to tell me that.' Alexander found that he was imitating some of Robert's mannerisms.

'You could have a good time if you go along with things; if you leave the servants alone. They run the place. They won't leave you alone if you interfere with them.'

'I see.'

'You've brought enough money with you?'

'Why do you ask that?'

'You've got to keep in with the servants here as I say.'

'I see. You're a servant, are you?'

'You could say that. For some purposes I am.' He put a hand to his jaw and scratched the side of his chin. The hall was quiet and the sound was audible. 'For a start, you are new here and you don't know where Gaughlin lives.'

'That's true. How could I know?'

'So you can't go and see him yourself, can you? And if you found your way to his house how do you know they'd let you in?'

'You were told to go and get the information from him. You are not being helpful.'

Robert shrugged his shoulders. 'I was told to go by them. But who are they? You don't know that. And they stated no time; Mrs Killinger said that your appointment was for nine; it's gone twelve now. What do you think your lateness will do for you? The longer you hang about arguing the longer you'll wait.' He looked down at his own feet. There was nothing in his tone of voice which suggested that he was in a hurry.

Alexander saw that his feet were bare. 'How much do you want?'

'You are not trying to bribe me are you? You didn't think I was standing here to get money out of you? Do you think we're corrupt? As I say, you have to keep in with the servants here.'

Alexander attempted to conceal his growing anger. 'You could regard anything I give you as a tip.'

'I like my tips given graciously.'

'Is that so?'

Robert pushed himself from the wall, walked over to him, and put a hand on his shoulder. 'Look, I'll go down to Gaughlin's for you. It's not all generosity on my part; I like to get out of a morning. I don't get much chance as a rule. But seeing that you've mentioned tips you might like to go to the kitchen and ask Mrs Killinger for an entry in the gratuities book.' The tone of his voice seemed candid. 'She'll sort you out on that score.' He yawned as he faced Alexander; then he walked lazily to the door, not glancing behind him. Alexander watched him from the hall. He saw him walk up a cinder track to a shed half hidden amongst shrubs.

Robert took the bicycle from the shed. He looked at the tyres. His every action was careful and indolent. He held the handlebars of the bicycle and stared out into the valley below the house. Then he threw a leg over the saddle and free-wheeled down the inclined drive.

Alexander still stood in the hall. His anger, far from evaporating, grew stronger. There had been something knowledgeably insolent about Robert's manner. Alexander would gladly at that moment have walked from the house and back to the station to wait for a train to take him back to the city. Where was his case? It no longer stood in the alcove; Apsleigh's assistant must have taken it away. Alexander walked down the passage to the kitchen. As he flung open the door Mrs Killinger and Apsleigh's assistant rose simultaneously to their feet, both of them looking at him without comprehension.

'Where have you put my case?'

'It will have been taken to your room,' said the man.

Mrs Killinger interrupted him. 'He has no room yet; not until the validation of the appointment comes through.'

'That's true,' said the asthmatic man. 'I had forgotten that fact. It'll be in the downstairs gentlemen's cloakroom.'

Alexander looked at their serious expressions. 'Would you mind getting it for me?'

Mrs Killinger raised her eyebrows and looked at her colleague.

'I'm leaving this house,' said Alexander. 'Kindly have my case fetched.'

Mrs Killinger began to walk to the door. 'Do you think that wise?' She made it clear that she would obey but only with reluctance. 'After all, you said you were summoned here and that you have an appointment.'

'I'd be pleased if you would do what I say. I can't remain here.'

Mrs Killinger suddenly turned to the asthmatic man. 'I know what it is. I could have told you. Robert has offended him.' She sighed, making no effort to move, but put her hands up to her head and fiddled with her hair, arching her back as she did this. 'I could have told you that we shouldn't have left him alone with Robert.'

Alexander was still very angry. 'How can you put up with him? He should be dismissed.'

Mrs Killinger's manner relaxed slightly. 'He is very lazy.' She looked at her reflection in the steamy surface of a mirror which happened to hang on the wall near where she stood. She smiled; Alexander, though he

29

could see neither her smile nor the mirror's reflection of it, could tell from the way she spoke that she was smiling. 'You shouldn't judge him too harshly on one meeting. He's strong; he's a help when there are heavy portering duties to be done. Besides, you might think differently of him, and make some allowances, if you knew his family background.' She turned from the mirror and smiled at Alexander almost coquettishly. 'You must not let him offend you. After all, you won't see much of him.'

The thought came to Alexander that, were he to return immediately to his city, he would certainly be questioned as to the nature of the course of instruction. If he returned now, how could he answer? Could he merely state that he had been somewhat badly treated by a few servants? What kind of answer would that be? More obliquely, what would the organizers of this course think when they came to hear (as assuredly they would hear) the servants' statement that a visitor had arrived but, although he had been invited to wait, had not deigned to attend the course?

'These are early days,' said Alexander. 'Perhaps I'm misjudging things.'

'You'll stay until things are sorted out, then?' asked the asthmatic man with an earnest slowness.

'I think it would be for the best.'

'I'm pleased to hear that.' The relief in Mrs Killinger's voice was very genuine.

Alexander spoke to conceal his embarrassment; he was aware that he had been vacillating and weak. 'Do you know anything about this course of instruction?'

'No, I don't.'

'Do you know how many other visitors have arrived? They might be attending it.'

'Well, only you have arrived. Perhaps you are the only one. Mr Gaughlin never mentioned that anyone had arrived while he was on duty. One would expect him to have mentioned any visitor.'

'I see.' He paused. 'Robert mentioned a thing he called "the gratuities book".'

30

'He would have done. You can't trust him.' She turned to her colleague. 'You see, I could have told you,' she said. 'He hasn't been here a minute and already Robert has been trying to get money off him.' As she spoke she walked over to the cupboard that stood on brackets screwed into the wall above Apsleigh's assistant's head. This man obligingly leaned to one side to allow her access to the cupboard. Mrs Killinger reached into the dark interior and brought down a book. She laid it on the scrubbed table. She began to turn the pages. 'It was very wrong of Robert to have mentioned this book. I wish he would exercise more care. I daresay – ' she addressed Alexander directly '– that he gave you the impression that all the servants were grasping? If that's so then I can only say how sorry I am. You have to understand him a little. After all, he never has any money. He gets through it so fast, what with his drinking and his girls – not that he spends much on them if he can help it.

'I doubt if he meant to be rude to you. He was probably acting hastily and without thinking.'

Alexander remembered the scene with Robert differently, but he said, 'I'll certainly give you something when I go. For my part I don't want to seem mean.'

Mrs Killinger smiled wholeheartedly at him. 'That's kind of you, to be sure, and we are all grateful to you. I said to Robert that you looked a respectable and kindly man and that he wasn't to offend you. But the way we do things here is slightly different; we try to be fair to all the servants and I hope you won't be offended.'

'Well, tell me about the way you do things.' Alexander's voice was heavily tolerant.

'It's like this. If you come to lodge here then you'll see in advance that various things will need to be carried out on your behalf. You are used to surroundings you can tolerate. You'll need your room to be cleaned regularly. Should you want a bath then the water for it must be boiled. Your food has to be prepared for you. Naturally you will need no fire in this weather, so that won't be necessary, but what will happen if they ask you to

31

stay here for a prolonged period? The overheads of the house have to be met.'

'I understood that I was on government business. Is this a hotel?'

'Of course not. These things are all provided in a government-run house; however, you will see that there are all kinds of errands and services which lie outside the procedures and policies as they are officially set down. In fact you might look at your own case; nothing has officially been done for you. But, at the same time, the servants have put themselves out on your behalf; that's quite understandable; you haven't been at all demanding. But you see how Robert has gone on a journey for you. You can envisage the effort which Mr Gaughlin will put into your cause even though he has never met you.'

Alexander looked up at the skylight. 'I see that. Look at the effort which has gone into taking my case from the hall to the cloakroom.'

'Now you follow me exactly.'

Alexander was uncertain whether Mrs Killinger was oblivious to the sarcasm in his comment or whether she had seen and had chosen to ignore it.

At that moment a bell sounded loudly in the very room in which they were standing.

A search for the source of the sound, which was at first unexpected, was made easy by the oscillations of the bell itself. The bell sounded noisily; the wire which pulled it jerked to and fro, now slack and now taut as it ran to a pulley and then up into a hole in the plaster ceiling.

Eight bells hung altogether, seven of them silent, dust and cobwebs lying over their mouths, but the eighth responded to the pull of its wire. A small shower of dust and plaster fell onto the linoleum of the floor.

'That's the master's bell!' Mrs Killinger looked up at it, twisting the fingers of her hands together. Then she hurriedly closed the gratuities book, and reaching up she thrust it into the cupboard and closed the doors.

32

Apsleigh's assistant began to pace the room with his mouth open as though to gain more breath; he was obviously agitated, clearly at a loss as to what he might do or how he might act.

The wire of the bell stopped jerking and the oscillations of the spring diminished. The bell was silent; it hung as statically as it had done before it had rung.

'Why is he ringing down?' Mrs Killinger had followed her colleague to the far end of the room as though she needed his support. 'I don't know how the bells work. Have the wires become twisted? That's happened before . . .'

They both looked at Alexander as though he had been the cause of the bell ringing.

'I'll go and find Mr Apsleigh,' said Mrs Killinger. 'He'll know what to do.'

Alexander was surprised at the number of servants in the house. Within a few moments of the bell's sounding at least a dozen people had congregated in the kitchen. They had entered as though with purpose; now they stood aimlessly, staring at the bell which had sounded or staring at one another in silent perplexity. Another group entered; their voices could be heard as they approached; as they came into the room they truncated their conversation. The first man in this group, a handyman to judge by his appearance, examined the wires which had caused the bell to sound. He seemed to need instruction in what he did; he cautiously touched the wire as though it were electrified. Someone called up to him as he stood on a chair. The silence was broken. The servants began to talk and to mill about the room.

Alexander alone was immobile in an atmosphere of unrest and ill-directed activity. He stood at the end of the tall room, underneath one of the skylights, watching the sudden disturbance which now filled the kitchen. Once he was approached by a man who thought that he, too, was a servant. He addressed Alexander in a manner which was peremptory and agitated; he could not make himself understood; his dialect was very broad and in his agitation he made no attempt to be comprehensible. Alexander was able to do no more than to look at him; he saw that he was a gardener for he wore mud-stained boots and a sacking apron upon which was printed, in a grey and faded stencil, the name and telephone number of a city seedsman.

'Where's Mr Apsleigh?' shouted a voice behind him; the words were clearly comprehensible though the source of them was difficult to determine.

Alexander, unable to participate in any way, found himself thinking what an absurd situation he had got himself into. Yet (and the thought came to him very clearly) it was no more absurd than many another occasion he had witnessed in the past. Perhaps any absurdity lay with him in his lack of understanding of what had happened and what was going to happen. Disjointedly (recalling a memory) he wondered how the Director's lecture at the Brownian Institute had gone. He remembered that the Director had the ability to speak fluently on any subject, even one which was outside his own experience; perhaps this indicated that fluency of speech might not necessarily be related to content. Alexander's gaze returned to the room where the servants were without direction. The thought came to him: were these inarticulate people without any order or hierarchy?

Although the ringing of the master's bell (or what they called the master's bell) had forced them to gather in this room, and had reduced them all to a state of collective agitation, the bell itself was unanswered.

Taking advantage of the confusion, Alexander made his way across the room, insinuating himself between the restless servants, until he stood underneath the cupboard which contained the gratuities book. He reached up and opened the doors. The cupboard was filled with miscellaneous things: over a dozen wrinkled damask napkins, a number of Britannia metal salt-cellars, a tarnished punchbowl with an equally tarnished ladle. Several books were stacked in a corner; copy books such

34

as might be provided for children at a school. He searched through them, aware that he was trespassing on the servants' property. He found the gratuities book. He held its spine in his hand; the book fell open naturally as though it had been opened previously in only one place. He saw a blank page that was headed by his own initial. The single abbreviation stood out, written in an illiterate hand. He wondered who had written it. There was no means of telling; the book was empty apart from that initial which he supposed represented himself.

He replaced the book in the cupboard and closed the door; he turned as he did this and saw that Mrs Killinger stood by his elbow, watching him. She smiled in her benign way, her face tilted to one side; she brushed the back of her hair with the fingers of one hand, a habitual action.

'What's the matter?' asked Alexander.

'Nothing is the matter, apart from the bell.'

'Well, why are you looking at what I am doing?'

'I was inquisitive. I saw you look into that cupboard.' She seemed to be too polite to mention that the cupboard had nothing to do with him.

'Yes, I was looking at the book you call the gratuities book.'

There could be no reply to this.

Alexander crossed his arms. 'I want to know the truth about what is happening here. I was called here to find a course of instruction and I cannot find it.'

'Yes, yes, you have told us that.'

The blandness of Mrs Killinger's manner perplexed him. 'I don't think I'll find it here,' he said. 'This is not what I expected.'

'You'd make a good servant,' said Mrs Killinger. She looked at him; she seemed to be sorry that she had made this remark. 'You're not going to the city, are you?'

'No; not until I have found the official course of instruction.'

'You make that sound very formal.'

'Formal?' Alexander looked beyond her at the

35

rudderless conglomeration of the servants, most of whom were again looking at the row of bells as though waiting for one to sound. 'I can see I'll get nowhere here! What is there upstairs?'

Mrs Killinger seemed alarmed. 'What do you mean?'

'I'm going upstairs.'

'I wouldn't do that.'

Alexander began to force his way through the press of people. 'I don't care about the appointment, or whether it has been validated.'

Mrs Killinger clutched his arm. 'No; you cannot go up there even if your appointment is in order. Think sensibly. If you were to go upstairs now they'd think that you were merely going up there to answer the summons of the bell.'

'What has the bell to do with me?'

They were standing in the dark passage which led to the hall and the staircase. Alexander turned to Mrs Killinger. 'I don't want to be rude, but I have been here waiting all morning. You know that as well as I do. Time does press; it presses heavily; nothing I have seen or heard has helped me in the least with what I have been told to do. All my enquiries have been unanswered or answered elliptically.' He saw that Mrs Killinger was no longer listening to him; she stared back into the room, peering up at the bell.

'Have you noticed the smell in that room?' Alexander was reluctant to touch her or to raise his voice, 'And why are these people milling about without any purpose? Why isn't that bell either answered or ignored altogether?'

'Listen to me a minute.' Mrs Killinger's face, as she turned, had the same earnestness which it had expressed when she had pointed out the meaning of the gratuities book. 'If you go upstairs now, you'll be mistaken for a servant. You must avoid that. If, in future, you mention who you are, then they'll quickly come to the conclusion that you are a servant pretending to be a visitor – merely because your first arrival coincided with the bell.' Seeing that her words were lost on Alexander, she began to explain herself afresh. 'You can't be expected to understand all that happens in this house, not all at once. You can't be expected to understand the attitudes of the servants from one cursory glance. After all, if you take some of the servants here . . .' She pointed through the half-open door at the gardener, the man with the sacking apron. 'He was born near this house. He spent his childhood in its precincts. He is older than I am. Yet you see that when a bell rings he is in total confusion and does not know how to act, or what to do: his dilemma is such that he comes to you for advice; perhaps he thinks you are a servant like himself, but perhaps more acquainted with the interior, because he has never seen you before. He mistakes you for an inner house-servant. You can see from this how easily these misunderstandings arise. I happened to see this; I wasn't being particularly inquisitive but one can't help seeing these things. Besides, I had taken a kind of interest in your welfare.'

'Why should you have done that?' Alexander had wished to follow the gist of her words, but the aimless activity of the servants was very distracting, and he had misheard her.

'Well.' Mrs Killinger looked down at the floor, silent in thought. She seemed to be listening to the ascendant voices in the hubbub. 'I can only say that we were pleased when you arrived. I remarked as much to Mr Apsleigh's assistant when I first saw you walking along the road and looking up at the house. He and I were standing at the window of the first-floor landing.'

'I see.'

'No; pardon me. Let me finish. We were standing at that window; it gives a fine view of the whole town. We saw the steam as the train arrived. We saw you coming out of the station gates and walking over the railway bridge.' She paused. 'I said to Mr Apsleigh's assistant, "Perhaps he is coming here. He seems to be unfamiliar with his surroundings." We were pleased when you arrived.'

'Yes, I'm not surprised. It wasn't long before the gratuities book was pointed out to me.'

'That's not the reason. You're always thinking of money.' She stopped talking and moved aside to allow another servant to enter the room; a chauffeur, perhaps, to judge by his uniform. 'Well, to be truthful, the gratuities book wasn't the whole reason, although I will say that Mr Apsleigh's assistant . . .'

The bell rang again. There was no doubt that it was the same bell. Every eye in the room looked up at it. Some of the servants stared with their mouths open and some stared with their mouths closed. In the middle of the room a group of servants scattered as though from a secret and guilty conversation.

'I shall go upstairs.' Alexander spoke with loud vehemence; a moment ago he had had to shout in order to make himself understood. Now his words were distinct, for the bell had stopped and a profound silence had fallen. His voice alone had spoken.

There was nothing he could do but leave by the dark passage. He felt the relaxation of the atmosphere and saw the relief in the servants' faces as he left.

They crowded round the door. It was plain that some of them were only inhibited from asking his advice by the presence of their silent colleagues.

He walked across the hall; they followed him. He could no longer see either Mrs Killinger or the asthmatic man.

He put one foot on the lowest tread of the stair. Ahead of him the brown linoleum stretched upward. He wanted to turn round; a dozen enquiries were on his lips, but he knew that if he uttered them it would be through cowardice. He wanted advice himself, but he had the suspicion that, were he to turn and question the servants, he would hear only surmise and rumour, or a truth tempered by the thought of the book they referred to as 'the gratuities book'.

When he was at the first landing of the stair he looked down. The hall below him was seen as a foreshortened rectangle. The upward-staring servants were seen as though from a considerable height; an untruthful impression, for there had hardly been twenty steps between the hall and the stair's turning. It was difficult to distinguish Mrs Killinger's face amongst the many faces, but he thought he saw her. Perhaps the false sense of distance was due to the fact that the servants, intent on peering over one another's shoulders, had inclined their faces to face an impossible elevation. It was difficult to tell.

'Wait.' The voice had no obvious identity. 'You have no authorization.'

It was clear that the speaker was reluctant to ascend the stairs. This induced Alexander to go on, but he was filled with trepidation: how should he have the temerity to climb the stairs when the speaker was clearly unwilling to do so himself?

What was there at the top? If there was anything to be afraid of, and something more than the breaking of an unknown code of protocol, why had Mrs Killinger stated that she had been in the habit of standing, with the asthmatic man, at the window of the higher landing?

The turn of the stairs was lit by a tall window. Beyond, the stairs changed their character. Now they were cantilevered out from the wall; they seemed unstable and unsafe; the drop from the painted iron balustrade was vertiginous and he kept to the wall in the same way that he had kept to the wall of an open stair in the dome of a museum which, in the course of his work, he had occasion to visit. Distantly, and from far below, he heard the sound of the bell sounding impatiently again.

The high landing was protected by a thin and insubstantial rail. Nothing led from it but a closed door and a single window. He turned to the window, classically proportioned and round arched, and walked across to it. Its sill was level with his chest. The clear undistorted glass showed the broad afternoon sky. He rested his hands on the stone sill and stared outwards; while he looked, he was aware of the drop behind him, as though the broad landing had not been there. Once, in his childhood, he had been taken up into the lantern tower of a mediaeval cathedral, and had suffered unbearable vertigo on looking down at the interior plummet to the crossing of the nave and the transepts, while, higher up and on the outside of the building he had been able to stand on the roof of that lantern and to look out across the flat landscape without any feeling of insecurity. Now, as then, he found it easier to look outwards.

The window looked out over the valley. As Mrs Killinger had said, it overlooked a remarkable prospect of the town. The drive of the house was seen as though from a vertical viewpoint, and beyond the drive was the road, the market square which Alexander recalled without detail, the station courtyard, the station itself with the two roofs and the footbridge. The platforms and the railway lines continued along the same direct and ruled perspective as though this window had been set to gain a premonitory view of any traveller who wished to reach the house. Alexander wondered why, when he had stood in the station courtyard, he had not looked upward and seen this very window. Perhaps this window had been hidden from sight because it was only one of many in the same tall house, as the house itself had been indistinguishable amongst a line of secretive nineteenth-century villas.

Someone was standing behind him. He turned, his back now to the window, and saw a figure distantly at the edge of the landing. This newcomer (Alexander thought of him as a newcomer, though he must have been standing in the shadow of some part of the landing long before Alexander's arrival) was dressed in a faded black suit which, it was increasingly apparent, had been tailored for an anatomy very different from that of the man who now wore it.

'Are you Mr Apsleigh?' Alexander asked the question as though he had intended a statement. His voice echoed down the stairwell.

'No.' His voice was interrogative: 'Have you met Mr Apsleigh?'

'I haven't.'

'I'm his secretary.'

Alexander resolved not to speak to him, but to wait and listen to what he had to say. But the man did not move; he leant back at the edge of the landing, his hands clasping the iron balustrade, uncaring or unaware of the drop behind him.

'That's a good suit you're wearing.' Alexander's voice contained nothing if not sarcasm.

'Do you think so?' He looked down at his own suit with surprise. 'It's fairly new, or so the man who gave it to me said. He had quite a large wardrobe of clothing, and . . .' He shrugged his shoulders. There had been elements of pride in his voice. The secretary began to examine the sleeves of his own coat, plucking at them with a finger and thumb, pulling out loose threads. 'The cuffs are scarcely worn.'

'That's very true,' said Alexander, though he saw that the man's suit was in the last stages of decrepitude. Alexander was leaning against the framework of the window; his posture was careless as though the secretary, because of his ill-fitting clothes and his vanity, had set him at ease and had given him an enhanced opinion of his own security.

It was perhaps this sense of superiority which allowed Alexander to question the man freely and even aggressively, as though the secretary were somehow responsible for the maintenance of order in this house. Alexander's questions were predictable: who were the servants? Who paid them? Where did they come from? Who was the master? What was the nature of the course of instruction to which Alexander had been invited? If the servants had authority in the house, as they claimed, why was there no apparent hierarchy or precedence? If they had authority, why had they been thrown into a state of indecisive consternation by the sounding of the bell? On the other hand, if they were

41

subservient, why had the bell rung unanswered?

The secretary listened to these questions with a polite quietness. Sometimes he smiled secretly.

'What amuses you?'

'You see some things in a very odd manner,' he said. 'That's of no importance.'

He listened to each question, pondering each one deeply. He answered thoughtfully, his voice soft and apologetic. From time to time he smiled again, amused at some inconsistency or other. One had the impression that he was committing some of these inconsistencies to memory as though for recounting in the future. He spoke, but his answers always left doubt. Some of the questions he parried in a straightforward manner. To some of them he replied by carefully pointing out the false premises upon which they were based. Some questions he elaborated so that they became diffuse and any possible answer vague and meaningless.

One thing alone was certain: this man who looked so ill-clothed had no mean brain. This single fact stood out as though in silent answer to all the questions which Alexander wished to ask him. The man wasn't answering his questions. What were his origins? He seemed to lack the blinkering servants' approach to unexpected events but none of the people downstairs could have looked more servant-like than he. Perhaps he was playing a part. If he were as intelligent as his conversational adroitness suggested, why should he have been so vainly pleased by Alexander's sarcastic comments about his dress? Had he been immured in this house for so long that he had forgotten the standards of the outer world? The interpretation was there to make but the facts were elusive.

'Who rang the bell?'

'Probably the master.'

'That is, the master of the house?'

'That's right.'

'Then why wasn't it answered?'

'Two reasons. Firstly, I say only that the bell was

probably rung by the master; it might not have been. That is a concrete reason. The important reason is that the servants are not expected to answer it.' He smiled to himself; it was possible that he was making this up as he went along. 'With all deference I must point out that you have only been in this house for a few hours; you can't be expected to know what the ringing of the bell signifies.'

'I know that when a master rings a house-bell, then it is a servant's place to answer it.'

'Normally that would be true.'

'Then why didn't it happen here?'

'One could argue that it wasn't an ordinary house-bell. Secondly, though the master is called the master and the servants the servants, it does not do to suppose that the servants are the master's servants. To say that would be to simplify the relationship between master and servant until it becomes meaningless. In many way the difference between the master and the servants as a body is the same as the difference between each grade of servants. When I use the word "grade" I don't imply hierarchical or financial differences. You will perhaps argue: "If the master knew that his bell was going to be unanswered, why did he bother to ring it?" and the answer to that is simply that he was demonstrating the order of the system. That is at least one interpretation, but I grant you there are others. And as for the ringing of the bell – you must have seen how they stared when they saw you begin to climb the stairs.'

'I noticed that.'

'Good. Why do you think they stared at you?'

'How should I know?'

The question had been rhetorical. 'They stared at you because the fact that you had no authorization to leave the hall to some extent negated the fact that you were not allowed to answer the bell.'

This proved to be too much for Alexander's patience. 'Why should I answer it? It's hardly my place. Look, I've had enough. The extortion of the gratuities book . . .'

'They mentioned that to you, did they?'

43

'They lost no time in doing that. I examined the page with my name on it.'

'They normally just use an initial.' While he was speaking he had walked away. Perhaps he had become bored but was too polite to show it. He ran his hand along the top of the door frame as though to check that it had been dusted. He examined his fingers and brushed the dust from them by wiping his hand on the lapels of his jacket. His attitude was preoccupied and meditative. When he next spoke it was as though for the sake of speaking. 'So you were called here to attend a course of instruction.'

'Yes, I was. I have a letter . . .' Alexander pulled the letter from his pocket and held it out. The envelope was already showing signs of wear; its folds were slightly soiled and its corners dog-eared.

'That's your letter?'

'Yes, it is. Read it; look at it for yourself.' He was aware that his voice was trembling; the fact that the echoes from the blank walls trembled also did nothing to calm him. He knew that he was on the point of revealing his mind to this man; perhaps he would have done so already had the secretary not given the impression that he was preserving this interview for later recall.

'I don't want to read your letter,' he said. 'I believe you. I can see the envelope. It's a very personal letter and it doesn't do to show these letters about without discrimination. Besides, I can guess what it says.' He closed his eyes. 'Do you really think I can give you directions?'

'You could give me advice.'

The secretary looked at him. 'I wish I could help you. I'd like to be able to.' He sighed and began to run his finger along the top of the door frame again. 'I can tell you one thing that you might do well to consider.'

'What's that?'

'It's only a speculative question based on the few things I know about you.'

Alexander began to laugh. 'What is it?'

44

The secretary's next words arrested that tense laughter. 'Have you considered that your course of instruction may already have begun?'

Alexander looked at him sharply. 'Is that a serious suggestion?'

The other man shrugged his shoulders. He began to rub his hands together, looking down at them while he did so. 'It was only a suggestion. What will you do now?'

'I'm not sure. I can't go back to the city because I don't know the questions they will ask me, let alone how I shall answer them. I can only keep on.'

The secretary nodded. 'You construed the letter to indicate something of direct personal significance to yourself. You have acted on surmises made from the letter.' He glanced at Alexander as though embarrassed for him. 'Now you say that it's too late to change the course of your action, though you must realize that it can never be too late for you to change the interpretation you put upon the letter.'

Alexander, who had started to pace the landing since it had been put to him that his course might already be in progress, stood in front of the closed door. 'What's in there?'

The secretary followed his pointing hand. 'You are very inquisitive,' he said, and then he lost interest in the door and leaned over the balustrade, peering down the stairwell.

'A man in my position has to be inquisitive,' said Alexander. 'Is that the only room on this floor?'

'No. There are other staircases.'

'Well, what's in that room?'

The secretary still stared down the stairwell. 'I'm not sure. The last time I had cause to go in there was some time ago. There was a man who used the place as an office. He had nothing to do with the household; he just had the room. I suppose that he must be employed by the government to have the room. He may have left. The room may have changed.'

'Did he live here?'

'He lived in that room, yes, as far as I know.'

'Did he rely on the servants for food?'

'I don't remember. It's been some time since I thought about him.' The secretary paused and lifted his head.

A row of red fire buckets, filled with sand, hung from the wall next to the stair-head. The secretary looked at them; perhaps their faded redness had caught his eye. He idly walked towards one, dipped his hand in, raised his hand and allowed the sand to trickle through his fingers. 'It's curious that you should ask about him. I think he did take his dinner and indeed all his meals in that room. It's a self-contained flat, you see; a water-closet and bathroom were made by panelling a corner of the room. Very convenient.'

'So this man was a guest in the house?'

'Yes, I think you could say that.'

'Perhaps I might see him.'

'That would be unusual. Besides, I have no idea whether he still lives in that room.'

'Well, I shall try to see him. I suppose he has an entry in the gratuities book?'

The secretary shook his head. He dipped his hand into the fire bucket again. He said nothing.

'Is there any procedure for seeing him?'

The secretary looked up. 'He used to have a servant; his own servant, not a member of the household. He arrived with his master. The servant, if I recall my facts correctly, used to live in an inn in the town. We never saw much of him except for the times when he fetched meals.' He looked at his watch. 'I must go.' He had reached the head of the stairs. 'Have you made your arrangements for eating?'

'No; not yet.'

The secretary began to walk down the stairs. 'I don't think you'll be able to eat here. Not at the moment.' He had reached the turn of the stair. 'For myself, I'd like to see you fed here . . .' He shrugged his shoulders. 'But you see how it is. One cannot fly in the face of authority.'

Alexander watched him. The broad landing seemed empty and tenantless. 'Wait, will you?'

The secretary paused; he glanced upward. Although he

was very distant Alexander caught a glimpse of his eyes. The secretary stood still. 'Yes; what is it?' His voice echoed in the stairwell.

'Come back a moment.'

The foreshortened form of the secretary stood immobile. He was reluctant to ascend. 'Look, I'd be pleased to help if I could do something definite.' He shook his head. He began to climb the stairs again. 'Anything I have to say will be of little help to you.'

When he reached the top of the stairs he was breathless, even though he had not climbed more than three quarters of the flight. 'You cling to your old standards as though they had an unalterable existence in their own right.' He tried to catch his breath while he said this; his hand was resting on the ornamental newel as though for support. 'If you want me to say anything further then you must not expect me to say the things you want to hear.

'You first met me not long ago, yet you thought that the fact of my old suit gave you a certain ascendancy. You saw me badly dressed and that gave you self-confidence.' He paused. 'I'm sorry for you. You were quick to judge. Perhaps I would have done the same thing myself; I never try to act the part of a judge. I feel a sympathy for you because you are in your predicament. Perhaps that gives me the right to feel my own superiority. Perhaps empathy would have been a better word; I don't know.

'All this comes back to a moment ago when you called me back up the stairs. If I could have given you advice I would have done, long ago, gladly, sparing the talk.'

'You are using words for the sake of it.'

'For the sake of what? For the sake of the words? For the sake of speech? For the sake of my own position and status in the house? Why should I use words like that?'

Alexander spoke immediately. 'Your whole attitude is false. I came up those stairs and I didn't know what I would find. I made some sarcastic remark about your suit and you reacted by treating me as though I had

47

praised you. My sarcasm was false but its reason was my insecurity. You had the benefit of knowing what you were doing when you replied.'

The secretary looked at his watch again. He looked up tolerantly. 'I see what you mean,' he said. 'I was, if you like, feeling my way.' He leaned on the balustrade.

Alexander saw that the condition of his suit was even worse than when he had first seen it. The lining was torn and the frayed black silk hung down. Perhaps the fabric was not so much worn as rotten.

When the secretary had left, Alexander turned to the window that faced the valley. The view was enough to occupy him for a while. It was at first impossible to take the view except as a composite whole, as though it were a picture seen distantly. Only later could he make out the grounds of the house as they sloped down to the road. Following the road his gaze was led to the town. To the left, amongst trees, stood the church. The clock-face on the tower, seen from above, indicated an unimportant hour. To the left of the road was a building with a complex roof of valleys and ridges; it might have been the town hall. Around it was a cluster of tiled roofs which intersected in a warm mosaic of orange rhomboids. Beyond the town hall was the slate roof of the railway station. There the perspective of distance started. The iron rails started out from under the glass platform roofs and ran on until the railway track was marked by hedges and trees where the valley met the plain.

The town was as ordered and as haphazard as any provincial town.

The house was silent. He had turned from the window and had sat beneath it on the floor. He began to take things from his pockets. He opened his diary and saw the sparse entries. Looking at them now it was easy to see how little the events had justified the past entries in the diary: perhaps the entries in the time ahead would hardly be worth their fulfilment. Yesterday he had recorded the fact of the course; the entry was brief and consisted of only one line of writing, and that written without any particular emphasis. Another person looking through the diary would certainly have failed to see the entry; the diary in itself gave no clue as to the fulfilment of what had been written. Alexander, idly examining the pages of his forward-looking diary (he had never been interested in the habit of recording past events), saw how little the eventuality could be forecast by the few words which had in the past been written only as an aid to memory.

A few hours ago he had thought that he, by coming here, had committed himself beyond any prospect of return until his goal had been reached. Now he wondered what the event would look like in retrospect.

The man who ascended the stair carried a tray, its contents hidden by a large dish-cover of faded pewter. He walked to the door and balanced the tray on his left forearm while he turned the handle. All this was done with skill; the metal tray must have been heavy and the dish-cover was a bulky antique thing. His face was preoccupied. He opened the door with some dexterity; he laid the tray on the surface of a table which could not be seen. He closed the door behind him.

The landing was again empty except for Alexander. It was, it seemed, a place where the silence was only heightened by people who passed it on their way to other places. The sun's track traversed the walls. In a few more hours it would be a shadowy vault.

The servant opened the door and stood on the landing. The tray he held now was identical to the one he had carried earlier.

'Come here a moment.' Alexander's voice, though not meant to be supplicatory (the reverse was true), stirred echoes which had a supplicatory quality to them.

The servant looked around the landing, standing still and searching it methodically with his eyes. It was growing dark and he could not have seen Alexander earlier.

The servant had seen him. The concentration shown

by his eyes was at variance with his impassive and expressionless demeanour. Perhaps his manner meant nothing; it might have been the result of an innate guardedness or the experience of a servants' training course. He began to walk towards Alexander. He looked down; then, as though he had seen something unusual he knelt beside Alexander and stared at his face as at a sick man's. 'Yes?'

Alexander had difficulty in speaking. It had been easy for him to call to the man across the landing, not knowing whom he called. Now that Alexander had seen him closely he was frightened by him. The single word had been clearly spoken with a preternatural distinctness emphasized by the silence of the place they were in. The word had sounded as though said to and heard by someone on the verge of sleep. Its very distinctness made it seem unreal.

The servant stared at him watchfully, his full face to him, his eyes unmoving. 'What do you want?' His voice was quiet but his words were very clearly enunciated. Alexander, looking at his face but avoiding his eyes, caught an imagined sight of what lay behind the expressionless manner, and saw the results of an experience which he had never undergone. This man was of Alexander's age (and indeed he resembled Alexander) but something had happened in his life to alter him. His inexpression showed knowledge and intelligence but no opinion. His calmness was hardly gained. All this for some reason made Alexander afraid of him.

Alexander had intended asking him for help, but this was not possible. He was quiet; he could not trust himself to speak without his voice trembling. He did not know how to say anything to the servant without provoking contempt: contempt which might never be expressed but which would always remain.

The servant, still waiting for the answer to his question, showed no sign of impatience. Alexander raised a hand and saw that it was unsteady. He locked his hands together lest this unsteadiness was noticed. He stood up, awkwardly, as though cramped; he brushed his clothes briefly with his erratic hands. He was conscious of his own fast pulse. The servant, unmoving, watched him. 'You're shaking,' he said. He began to stand.

Alexander felt that he was about to faint. 'You must hold me in contempt,' he said, half to himself. He was hardly aware that he had spoken the words.

The servant considered this. He looked discreetly away. 'No.'

'I'd like a word with your master,' said Alexander faintly.

The servant nodded his head; he walked to the window and looked out, beyond the town, to the distant horizon of the plain.

'If it could be arranged,' continued Alexander. He looked at the servant's back. The man's very presence disturbed him. He found that he was still holding the diary in his hands. He tried to put it back in his breast pocket but his hand jerked and he dropped it. He left it where it was – he could not stoop because of a sudden vertigo.

The servant turned at the sound and looked at Alexander briefly. 'What name shall I give him?' His voice, for the first time, echoed a sadness. He spoke as though he was aware of the agitation his presence had caused.

Alexander wished above all things that he had not asked to see the servant's master. He wanted to say this; it no longer mattered whether his voice shook; in his present fear he was not afraid of contempt. He tried to speak but could not.

The servant stood in the semi-darkness for a little while longer and then he walked to the door. He still carried the tray.

His departure did nothing to calm Alexander. When he returned, Alexander was still on the landing and his diary still lay on the linoleum. 'He asks you,' he said, from the doorway, 'to allow him ten minutes.' He walked down the stairs.

51

When he was alone Alexander was aware of a growing anger which began to dispel his fear. He walked across the landing, jerkily picked up his diary and replaced it in his pocket. The faintness and the rapid beating of a pulse in his head had gone. 'I'm a free man! I can't be terrorized like this!' He began to descend the stairs, losing his caution, running down the steep flights.

The hall stretched away emptily. He was hungry but knew that his hunger would evaporate at the sight of food.

In the kitchens the saucepans were still steaming and the air was thick and moist. He closed the door behind him. He had not thought this room welcoming when he had seen it before, but now it seemed a homely room, able to reassert the presence of a rational world physically removed from the high and insecure landing.

Mrs Killinger was talking to the asthmatic man. There was something about the manner of both that gave the impression that they had been arguing and had only just reached an unsatisfactory agreement. Mrs Killinger's voice was sharp and very much in contrast to the wheezing breathlesssness of the man. They were discussing domestic finance. Robert was in the room, too, but he took no part in the talking. He leaned against the edge of the dresser, at ease, his muscular arms folded. There was a totally unconscious gracefulness in his indolence. He stared at the glass of one of the skylights, watching the formation of drops of condensation.

All three of them ignored Alexander's entry. Only when he sat down in a chair did Mrs Killinger turn to him, resentful, or so it seemed, of this little liberty he had taken.

'So you've come back to us! You've been up there almost the whole day. Weren't you interested in the way your interests were handled?'

'What do you mean?' After his recent experiences it did not seem to matter what he said.

'Robert's been down to Mr Gaughlin's for you. He'll

52

try again tomorrow; he's offered to do that for you.' She paused, looking at him. 'So you shouldn't judge people on first acquaintance.'

'I'm sure you're right. I'm grateful. Mr Gaughlin wasn't in, then?'

'He isn't in, no.' She smiled, apparently to put him at his ease, but this time her smile was forced and artificial. 'Whatever's the matter with you? You're white.'

'Nothing's the matter.'

'The validation is nothing to worry about, if that's what you're thinking. You must have a strong sense of propriety if you're still unduly concerned about that! There's not much you can do, after all, except to let things take their course.'

'It wasn't that. I felt faint, suddenly.'

Someone else had entered the room.

The newcomer stood quietly until Mrs Killinger had finished the sentence she was speaking ('I doubt if you've eaten anything today,' she had said), and then, not moving from his place by the door he said, his voice unremarkable, 'I came to remind you of your appointment.' He did not wait for a reply before he left the room.

'As I was saying . . .' (Mrs Killinger had registered her acknowledgement of the message-bearer's presence only by her impatience) '. . . it's no wonder you feel faint. You've had nothing to eat.'

Robert had been more observant. 'What's the matter with you? Who was that?'

Alexander turned towards him.

Robert had uncrossed his arms; he stood straight, his legs apart. He jerked his head in the direction of the door. 'Who was that? Is he a relation of yours?'

'I don't know who he is.'

'What's he got over you?' He looked about the room briefly. 'Something's happened to you since you went up when the bell sounded. You can tell us; we can keep a secret.'

'Nothing's the matter.'

Robert put the fingers of his hands in his pockets. 'He

53

has something over you, though. You can't deny it.'

'Don't question me about that!'

'Don't question me about that!' Robert was a good mimic. 'You sat shaking there in that chair like a school kid in an empty room with the bully.' His voice showed his perplexity. 'You were never like that before. I'm sorry for you, that's all.'

'I don't know who he is except by hearsay.'

Robert looked down at him in silence. 'Ah! Naturally.' He shrugged his shoulders. 'I don't know him myself, but I've seen him before. Not one of us. I've never heard anyone speak of him badly.'

'I'm not speaking of him badly.'

Robert ignored this. 'Mrs Killinger, who was he? Do you know him?' His voice was loud.

'He's only a servant to someone on the first floor. That's all I know about him.'

'He's not a servant to the master of the house, then?' asked Alexander.

'No, of course not!' cried Mrs Killinger. 'The master's servants know each other well because of the system in which they work. He has no place in it; if he did we'd know his name and everything about him.'

Alexander only half listened to this. It was time for the appointment he had requested.

When he had closed the kitchen door behind him he heard the three people inside talking simultaneously. The asthmatic man, the man who was the least talkative in Alexander's presence, now seemed voluble and his voice was dominant.

The door, which he saw to be slightly ajar as he approached it across the darkening landing, did not lead to a room directly (though the memory of the exterior geography of the house suggested that it should do) but to a long corridor which led into distance. The floor, like the other floors, was laid with brown linoleum and the walls were gloss-painted; brown for the first four feet

54

and cream for the upper two thirds. Between the two glossy colours was a line of black, perhaps two inches wide. Intermittently along the length of the corridor, stacked to one side, were cardboard boxes, tea-chests, piled books and bundles of music manuscript. Paintings, framed and unframed, were stacked on top of each other. The disposition of these things argued not so much the use of the corridor as a lumber room but as a convenient place for the temporary storage of belongings prior to removal.

These belongings had been stacked along the corridor with care and in some kind of order. Several packing-cases were full; beyond the packing-cases there were tea-chests stamped with the name of a removal company. On looking along the corridor it became clear that the removal company had left insufficient chests and cases; the leatherbound books at the extremity of the corridor were tied with twine; the larger canvases had been merely gathered together and heaped on top of the piles. These things were undisturbed; they were covered with dust. Perhaps the removal company had never arrived.

He made his way along the corridor. Initially he walked quickly, anxious to reach the further door and to avoid any prolongation of the unwelcome interview. When he was closer to that further door he grew reluctant to knock at its panels and began to look at the packaged lumber. He stood directly beneath a skylight. The poor remains of the downward falling daylight caught a pile of canvases which lay on a muffled library of dusty books. The canvases were half leaning against the wall and the outermost of them presented itself to his eye.

The canvas which arrested his attention portrayed the head of a figure which was undoubtedly intended to be a saint, but the thing which attracted him was not as much the subject of the picture but the fact – and this was obvious at the moment he first saw the canvas – that the picture itself was only the detail of a larger work. The representation was simple; the painting showed a saint, viewed in a strict and uncompromising profile. The face stared downwards. The curious lack of perspective indicated that the painting was early, or that the painter had abrogated perspective in order to make some point which was not obvious. The saint stared downwards and the face held an expression which combined anger, disquiet and even fear; the mouth was open and the teeth were bared. He looked at the painting: it had taken his imagination. He knew, or thought he knew, the intent of the painter. He knew (from the very idiom in which the image was depicted) that the portrayed saint was Saint George. The dragon was not there: the head of the saint alone filled the canvas, staring downwards, full of revulsion and fear, but in the interpretation the imagined surroundings were there. It needed little imagination to see the dragon and to see the saint's sword-arm upraised; it needed little imagination to see the frightened charger with mane flying and with eyes filled with animal fear and nostrils wide with the breath of animal exertion. Yet, despite the symbolism, the only pictured thing was the head of the saint. The legend followed.

Alexander, as he looked at this picture, this detail which might have been barbarously carved from a great canvas, knew that it was only his own upbringing that had allowed him to perceive it as the image it was, but as he looked at the picture in the failing light he saw that his first interpretation was not the only one which could be made, nor even perhaps the most obvious. The head of the saint was shown; that was a necessity. All else was speculation. The imagined dragon could have been any adversary, real or unreal; the frightened mount, imagined as it was, could have been any support and the sword which was seen in the mind's eye could have been any form of defence.

Once seen in this light the painting was a very different thing. It was no longer necessary to believe that it was a depiction of a saint. The image might have represented any man in a fearful extremity, even one which had no traditional comfort of known victory.

He still held the painting when he knocked at the door.
He was told to enter.

The room was large. The gaze was met by the window,
a high-arched casement which occupied most of the far
wall and which extended almost from the floor to the
plaster frieze that ran below the ceiling. There was no
furniture in the room except for a chair. In this chair sat
a man who leaned forward, engrossed in a thoughtful
examination of the town below. As he leaned forward he
appeared to be enframed by the window; from the back
of the room, near the door, the size of the window made
the bare room and the town almost contiguous, so that
the man who sat in the chair might have been engrossed
in something that was happening on the floor of the room
rather than in something that was happening out in the
valley.

Alexander walked across the room until he stood by
the chair. He followed the man's gaze to the valley and,
beyond, to the town where the lights of the station
glowed. A few people were walking across the square.
The street lamps flickered into yellow light in lines and
in rows.

The man in the chair turned to him briefly. His manner was preoccupied; perhaps something that was happening outside had interested him. 'I see you've arrived.
Close the door.' He muttered these phrases quietly,
minimizing interruption. 'I was told that you wanted to
speak to me.'

Alexander returned to the door and pushed it shut.

'I see you're holding a picture.' He had raised his
voice; he had stood up and now had his back to the
window as though he had dismissed it. 'Is that one of the
paintings from the passageway?'

'Yes, it is.'

'Why did you bring it in here?' He sounded
exasperated. 'I don't want it back in here. It's a painting
which belongs to my predecessor. Most of those things

57

out there belong to him. When I came I had them piled out there in the hope he might come back for them. They cluttered the place.' He arched his neck to look at the canvas. 'Turn it towards me.' He paused. 'You've found that one, have you? I'm surprised you can look at it with complacency.'

'It's only a representation of Saint George.'

'It certainly is not. It doesn't represent any saint. What did you wish to see me about?'

'I received a letter yesterday.' He was aware of the baldness of this; he found that he could not be bothered to choose a better phrase. He saw that the man who faced him was not a tall man; he was shorter than Alexander and his own servant would have dwarfed him.

'Did the letter ask you to attend a course of instruction?'

'It did.' Alexander looked at him more closely, wondering how he could have known this. 'I have it here. Do you know anything about this course?'

'Well, let me have a look at the letter first.'

Alexander took it out of his pocket. At first he had a certain reluctance to hand it to a total stranger.

Perhaps the stranger felt his reluctance. 'May I read it?'

'Certainly,' said Alexander, raising his voice as though he wished to deny to himself the presence of that odd reluctance.

Alexander watched him as he read it. He felt now that the letter was not explanation enough; he began to interpolate phrases: perhaps he felt a sudden apprehension that this man, who by his own admission knew of the existence of the course of instruction, might put him down as being half-hearted or insincere. 'I thought . . . I was beginning to think . . . that the whole thing was a fabrication, a summons without a point.' He paused. 'Nobody apart from yourself seems to know anything about it in this house.' He was aware that the letter was being read with the concentration of experience. 'I had no idea whether it is a suggestion or a command. It mentions the course; no more than that.'

58

'It says nothing more than that,' said the quiet man with slight irony in his voice. 'It is the usual letter, broadly speaking.' He looked up at Alexander, his manner quite animated. 'You are lucky that you have the letter. It's concrete evidence; you always have it to refer to. Some people are summoned by other means. If one has the misfortune to be telephoned one has no proof of summons at all. In time one mingles the fact of any message with the fiction of one's interpretation of it.'

'Many people have been called, then? And the course is officially recognized?'

'You put those questions as though they were statements which were both true.' He chose his words with care. 'Many people are called; I see them when they find their way here. As for the course, that must be recognized; the existence of the summons proves that.' He began to speak more rapidly. 'It always disturbs me, this reference to an "official course of instruction". People make mistakes and come here, expecting help. It's possible that they have been misguided or have mistaken some point of protocol – perhaps they have antagonized one or more of the people they relied upon for information. Sometimes in their attempt to placate and bribe their money has run out. They seem to arrive here. I was not aware of any of this when I took my present position and at first I was loath to see them, but I couldn't carry on like that. You may be an exception; I know nothing about you and the last thing I would wish to do is to attempt to fit you into a category, but with the general run of the recipients of letters – they are often both disorientated and without money – I found I had to do something. One has to take each arrival as it comes; each is so different that any set guide-lines would probably be of no help.'

'You make it seem as though there were no official course of instruction! Surely those letters aren't sent out at random, to people chosen by chance, making them travel across the country and interrupting their lives!'

'Of course there is a course. It's implicit in each

letter,' he said after he had thought for some time.

'But you have no other evidence for its existence than that? Do you know where it is held?'

'No, I don't, otherwise I would have told you before now. Because you and people like yourself have failed to find the course doesn't mean that it doesn't exist. In fact it only strengthens one's suspicion that it does. Some would even say that it must be a very paltry course were it capable of being stumbled on by accident. You have to know what you are looking for in these things.

'The letter tells you nothing apart from the invitation, or summons, and the fact that you are invited to the course, and a date and a time and a place. That's all it can tell you unless you have some further information or further insight. They used to say – those who had been searching for some time – that they sometimes had a spurious feeling that they were already attending it because of some event, or thought or inner feeling of conviction . . . I don't know. I can only piece together the things other people tell me; I have never received a letter. My knowledge is second-hand.

'The recipient of a letter always seems to be hampered by the confusion of prior experience. All new occurrences and experiences are seen and hastily viewed against comparable things from the past. Take your own example. Before you came in here you stood in the passageway and happened to see a painting. You would have found it disconcerting and the idea it conveyed uncertain had you not put it down as a representation of Saint George. Even had it represented the saint, the meaning of the painting would have been inexact and tenuous. Gelasius emphasizes the fact that Saint George was a man of whom almost nothing was known. In effect the memory you seized upon to help you was only a collection of legends and probable myths.' He looked at the painting again. 'It's strange that you should have found an identity between that canvas and the saint. I suppose it was the downward stare and the fearful expression which suggested it to you. It is curious.

60

The face is the face of a man in conflict; there can be no doubt of that.'

'What does it represent, then?'

'Only a local legend. By itself it doesn't capture the imagination. I suppose you thought the painting ancient?'

'I did. I thought that it had been cut from a larger canvas.'

'Not so. I believe that it was painted by my predecessor.'

'Why did he paint a halo round the head of the figure?'

'How should I know? I have no real insight into my predecessor's mind; I only met him once, and that was when I was being shown round the room. I wasn't particularly interested in him then.' He paused. 'And as for the halo, one can only conjecture the reason for it. Perhaps he felt that the subject, because of his struggle, deserved elevation; I don't know.'

'Then the picture has no religious significance whatsoever, despite all the marks which suggest the contrary view?'

'You could debate that point forever and get nowhere. Neither of us knew what was in the painter's mind. You could put a case either way. It would be easy to argue that there is a religious purpose to the painting, particularly in view of the fact that in the earliest available version of the legend we are not told whether the adversary is spiritual or physical. We can only guess the nature of the adversary; whether it has its origins in the man's mind or arises from outside him. The legend is simple, and it would have been better had it remained simple. As it was, in the usual way of things, simplicity was not enough because it demanded too much thought. Instead of the universal "adversary" a range of substitutes grew up; madness, sickness, a wronged brother, a beast, an archangel. Each version of the simple tale twisted it for the purposes of some cause or other . . . a church, a system of government, a system of moral teaching. In the original version there is nothing that leads one to suppose that the man is good and his adversary evil, and no evidence exists to support the contrary view. The legend is held and to my mind purposefully so.'

'Do you remember it?'

He smiled slightly; he had expected the question. 'I think I do, but I couldn't recite it without unintentionally putting a gloss of my own on it. That would perhaps be unhelpful.'

'You could try.'

'Very well. But it will not be the original.

'A man was pursued all his life by an adversary. In the beginning, before he was able to reason, he did not know that he was being pursued. In his adult life he was intermittently aware of his pursuer; at night, in times of silence, under the heat of the sun, while he worked, and, later, when he was in the company of his fellow men. Finding no refuge he fled before his adversary until he came to a mountainous country and, unable to fly further, he stood and faced his adversary.

'That is the version as I see it. It may be salutary to note that even in this corrupt version there is no mention of the possibility – and it's a popular supposition – that the man may have perished after facing his adversary.

'The version I have told you has lost its simplicity; the original makes no mention of certain words, like "all his life", "adult life", "intermittently aware", "at night", and all the other definite statements. The words, "pursuit", "pursuer" and "adversary" are, strictly speaking, accretions. Unless words like these are used, though, the idea of the legend is impossible to convey. All words have bias. The ones I have chosen are unhelpful.'

'I see no point in it.'

'Perhaps there is no point in it, except for the fact that it can no longer be recited as it was originally written.'

Alexander looked at him. 'What has it to do with me?'

'Why should it have anything to do with you? Are you falling into the old game of interpreting everything in the light of your own position?' He began to walk back to the window. 'I suppose it is possible to imagine a parallel with your letter.' He said this under his breath.

'Look back to your letter. How did it strike you when you first received it? You must have had some premonition of an importance which was beyond the words. Perhaps you felt that, as in the story I have just told you, the sense was being impeded rather than being helped by the words. Surely something like that must have been apparent. After all, no-one would have acted as you did because they had received a letter like that.'

'I don't know whether I agree with you or not,' said Alexander. 'The letter certainly did fill me with disquiet, and it's a fact that that feeling has grown. Why it affected me so strongly I have no idea.'

'Good. At least you are not making excuses for your behaviour. Do you know that you are unusually honest? Most recipients find difficulty in facing the truth and throw up a barricade of plausible fabrications for the arrival of their message. With time these fabrications become interwoven with the message. You are speaking plainly when you say that the letter filled you with disquiet; I can see it in you now. You reveal more to me than perhaps you realize. I put this to you: had your state of mind been slightly different, or had that letter arrived a day sooner or later – indeed, had it arrived at any other moment than the ordained moment – you would have not experienced that disquiet. The letter would have been torn up; you would have carried on in the routine of your life.'

Alexander began to walk up and down the room. 'This is empty reasoning,' he muttered, but at the same time he knew the other man's words to have been perceptive and probably truthful.

'Empty? It's not even reasoning.'

'Then why are you saying these things? They're abstract and useless. And as for that fable: you might have invented it as you were speaking.'

The man said nothing. He sat in the chair and resumed

63

his scrutiny of the town. His manner was so distant that Alexander wondered whether he had offended him. This appeared not to be so; after a few minutes he turned, his chin resting on the knuckles of his right hand. 'Surely I've been of some help. Have I given you nothing to think of?' He looked tired, as though he had not slept well for many nights. He seemed to have difficulty in recognizing Alexander, who stood at his side gazing vacantly through the glass of the great window. 'Keep that painting. Perhaps you don't see the despair which lies upon its subject.' He looked at the painting again. 'Against all that,' he said, suddenly, 'perhaps one learns far more of the painter than one realizes. One wonders what the true subject would be, were it to be stripped of all myth and all the gloss of emotion. One wonders if there is a subject at all; perhaps at the heart of it there is only a principle. Like others he may have chosen to try to make the principle intelligible by garbing it in myth, and so constructing an object which might run in its prescribed course to provide an example, or to be a guide. Others (they tend not to be painters) choose to generalize the principle in order to understand it, and in so doing they create a code which represents utility and morality. All this being said, it is quite clear that in both cases the original principle is concealed by the processes which would reveal it.' He still looked at the picture. 'He was,' he said, softly, 'given to the preoccupation of a man who sees more difficulties than perhaps there are. I'm reading too much into it. Perhaps it only shows his state of mind at the time he painted it. It's possible that it doesn't represent a sequence from the legend at all. Perhaps it only shows an inner struggle.'

'I'll keep it,' said Alexander. He waited, but the other man said nothing. 'Where is he now?'

'My predecessor? He left here long before he reached his retirement. I was told that he had a malignant condition, but that was only hearsay. He looked ill on the one occasion I saw him. He was due to send back for his belongings, so they told me, but he has never returned. After waiting for what seemed an appropriate time we had a few bonfires out in the yard with the more useless of his belongings.'

'Did he tell you that legend?'

'Why do you ask that?' He seemed surprised. 'No; he told me nothing about himself. He showed me round the room, and, as you can see, that didn't take him long. The legend is, as far·as I know, a local one. Perhaps it has survived because it has local relevance. When you visit the town you'll see how it is interpreted. Here and there, in unexpected places, you'll find representations of sequences from it, painted according to the hue of the painter's mind. I have been told that there is, in one prominent public place, a fresco which depicts the man at peace, before he is aware of his pursuer (indeed, to mention the possibility of pursuit sets an unintentional supposition on my part which is certainly not recorded in the fresco itself). That is, I believe, the only fresco. You may come across paintings. Some show him at the initial moment of his apprehension of the presence of a pursuer. Some attempt to show that the adversary does not necessarily pursue him, and that his pursuer is not necessarily his adversary or enemy. Others do not show that side of his life at all, showing as they do his life at home with his family, or alone in prayer; they seem to show him as though he had passed his life in ignorance of any adversary, as though an adversary did not exist. There has over the years been some stylization of the face, for he is always recognizable. The perspectiveless and falsely mediaeval manner might, apart from the ambiguity of his circumstances, have made a stereotype of him. One has to admit that it's difficult to see any significance in some of these paintings; on the other hand, if that is so, why is the legend so frequently use as a source of inspiration? Why do the same suppositions and presumptions occur and recur?' He had been speaking in a low voice as though he had been speaking to himself. 'Where are you staying the night?' His voice had a vestige of formality.

'They won't have me in this house,' said Alexander, promptly. 'That would risk them "flying in the face of authority". I'd thought about staying at the inn near the station.'

'The man who mediated in your appointment stays there.' He said this with the same tone of formality.

'He is your servant?'

'I've never regarded him as a servant.' The sitting man found the concept out of place. 'He isn't a servant.'

'What is he then?'

'He came here two years ago.' He seemed to be reluctant to speak, as though aware that he might be giving away a confidence. 'He came here when he was twenty. He had been summoned to attend a course of instruction; he had been called by telephone.' He spoke rapidly, before thinking, as though he had not intended this information to be known. 'He received no letter. He had searched the town for several weeks before he found this house; he was a long time in the house before he came here. When I first saw him he was angry and silent; angry with the authorities who had summoned him and who then did not appear. He was angry with the people downstairs. He had antagonized them; his anger had become broadened and encompassed all whom he met; he was truculent and ready to be angry with me. He had difficulty in telling me about his telephone call. Time had so distorted the message in his own mind that he no longer had a clear knowledge of what it was about; hence his ill-directed anger.

'You have seen what false interpretation may be made of the written word. In his case it was the greater because he had had no written message. His own distortions of half-forgotten fact and his own growing anger had so coloured his summons that it no longer bore any relation to the original.

'Besides, he told me that he had received the telephone message . . . and it was a message; he could not query it in any way. He said that it had been dictated to him by someone who did not understand it, in the small

66

hours of the morning. He told me that he had looked at his bedside clock at the moment the telephone rang; it had been something after three o'clock. He had been asleep; he had not shaken off his drowsiness when he took the message and the messenger rang off.' He glanced frankly at Alexander. 'You ought to remember that if you are ever worried for yourself. You can reflect on your good fortune. You, at least, can always go back to the fact of the written letter, and you may re-examine it and interpret it at will.'

Alexander stood at the centre of the room. He was directly behind the chair. He saw as though below him (and enframed by the window) the figure of the other man. 'This makes no sense to me. You are fooling with words. All the time you have been speaking in tangents, grasping the first idea that comes into your head.'

The other man seemed suddenly fatigued. 'You might consider leaving me.' There was no mistaking his weariness; he was behaving like a man who attempts to speak after taking a strong sleeping-drug. 'Here's your letter.' He held it out as if glad to be rid of it.

'I shall go back to the city. I've had enough of this.'

'Go, then, if you can. But first; tell me why you came so far? Why did you not tear up that letter and throw it away the first moment after you had read it?'

Alexander scowled at him, oblivious of the fact that he looked frail and seemed to be on the edge of sleep. 'I never knew what I was in for. Give it me; I'll get rid of it now.'

'Get rid of it now? No; use your sense; at least keep it until you find that you can do without it.'

Alexander reached forward and took the letter, grasping it from the other man's hand, momentarily surprised at how loosely the man had held it. Clutching it between his fingers he ripped it in two and then again and yet once more. He crumpled the fragments. 'Make what you can of it now,' he said. He threw the pieces of paper onto the floor. 'I don't want your empty talk. I don't want anything else you offer me.'

At the door he had no intention of looking back, but the desire to do so was insurmountable. He stood at the door, his hand on the latch, and he looked back at the room. It was exactly as it had been when he had entered it. The other man sat in his chair. Alexander saw the futility behind his own action; all he had done had been to look foolish.

The sitting man looked out of the window and the pieces of paper were strewn unregarded at his feet.

He walked out of the house and stood beneath the porch. The evening was still light; it was not as late as he had thought. The sun had set behind the hill but the sky reflected a soft redness. The fact that it was not yet night – he had expected the valley to be in near darkness when he had opened the door – gave him a premonition of freedom.

He looked at the valley, the hedged green fields, the hanging copses, the farm cottages on the further slopes. The upland moor that lay across the summit of the hill beyond the valley was reddened by the horizontal rays of the sun. The town, from the church to the hospital which might once have been a workhouse, lay beneath him in the comparative darkness of the valley-floor. All that he saw conveyed the impression of fixed order.

Alexander remembered the attitude of Mr Mause; perhaps he understood, or thought he did, Mr Mause's feelings as he had, that morning, stood beneath the porch.

He left the porch, suddenly, aware of the time, and he walked down the drive to the road. He forgot his hunger in a new vigour. The town square was empty and he met no-one; lights were on in the windows of the civic buildings. Further down the hill the roofs of the station were black against the glow of the platform lamps.

In the booking office the clerk looked at the departures board. He walked to the window, his tread dismal on the bare wooden floor. The hall was silent except for the rapid ticking of a white-faced clock which was prominent against the dark woodwork. The clerk stared along the empty platform where the geraniums bloomed in their tubs beneath the nameboards. 'You've half an hour yet, sir.'

'Half an hour,' murmured Alexander, following the clerk's eyes and looking at the empty platform. 'Is there a refreshment room on the platform?'

'Not at this time of day.' He looked at the ticket that lay on the wooden counter. He picked it up. 'This is a cheap rate. It's not valid on this train.'

For some perverse reason Alexander had half guessed this to be the case. 'They didn't tell me that when I bought it.'

'Perhaps you weren't clear as to when you were returning.'

He found that he had no particular wish to undertake another erratic train journey. He was afraid of the questions which his colleagues would ask about the course which he had never attended. As well as this he doubted whether he had enough money to buy another ticket without going to a bank.

He looked round at the diminishing perspective of the glass roof and the platform beneath it. The station was peculiarly vacant; he found it difficult to believe that he had ever alighted here this morning. His journey now seemed to be very much in his past; something which he had done as a youth. His recollection of it suggested that it had happened long ago. Perhaps this illusion was due to the air of remoteness that filled the station, as though its very platforms waited under sentence of closure.

'Eleven-ten will be your first chance to travel with that ticket.'

Alexander did not reply immediately, but looked out at the station buildings. When he turned to the clerk he found that the man was closing the window of the ticket office, perhaps out of the wish for privacy. Alexander left the station and walked up the drive to the town. He walked round the empty streets for half an hour, pausing to look into unlit shop windows, uncertain as to what he might do. During his walk he passed beneath the wall of the church. The windows, coloured with fragmentary stained glass, were lit from within. The rich light was welcoming. Alexander listened at the door, thinking that a service might be in progress: why else would the church be lit? The building was silent.

The white interior of the church was lit by fluorescent tubes which hung from the beams. The light was the cold afternoon light of a winter's day. At the eastern end of the building, beyond the whitewashed chancel arch, a brass alms dish rested on a wooden communion table. There were no other religious symbols. The windows, giving such a rich and warm light outside, were featureless when viewed from within. The contrast gave rise not so much to disappointment as surprise, and a feeling of deception. The building itself was ancient but the interior was white with lime-wash on new plaster.

Alexander began to walk down the aisle without purpose, for he knew that there could be nothing of interest; the building's interior had yielded its blankness to his first glance and there was nothing left. It needed imagination to remember that it was a church; in the cold light the little organ, the lectern and the pulpit might have been exhibits in a museum or articles stored in a warehouse. The pews, varnished with a sticky varnish, seemed unsuited to a devotional purpose. Alexander was alone in the building. He had been attracted by the light which had streamed out through the stained glass of the deeply recessed windows. The fact that the representations of the figures were incomplete (as though the fragmentary mediaeval glass had been reconstituted into modern panels) did not influence the character of the warm and coloured light. He had been surprised at the starkness of the interior when he had entered. The surprise was momentary. Had the lighting been softer, had the walls been hung with tapestries and texts and had there been the faint smell of extinguished candles, the church's interior would have been very different; a new atmosphere could have been created by material change and any deception might not have been noticeable.

The north chapel had no altar and its clean flagstone floor was an open expanse without pews or chairs. He stood in this chapel, his eyes following the perspective of the joints of the flagstones. He saw the vast picture which hung from the wall.

The picture was dark; perhaps its lead pigments were darkening still. It was well lit by the cold overhead light which showed the sagging of the unstretched canvas in its frame and the cracks in the paint and the layers of varnish. The subject was more elusive. It portrayed a standing man. It was not clear whether he was standing in a blank and featureless place, or whether his surroundings were amorphous and confused. His hair and his clothing were dark but it was impossible to guess their original colour. His expression was indeterminate. The stance of the figure appeared to show a sense of motion, as though the figure paused, rather than stood inertly, as he had first supposed. Continued examination did not help him to tell whether the figure was poised for flight or for some other action. It was easy to read impressions and circumstances into the painting. Alexander saw that the figure apprehended an ill-defined threat; at the same time he was aware that another observer might easily come to a different conclusion.

He was reminded of the legend which had been told him. He stared at the painting. Only after a time did it occur to him that the head of the figure was peculiarly defenceless. He looked for a chair; despite the darkness of the painting he wished to examine, more clearly, the medium which had given rise to that suggestion of defencelessness.

The chapel was shadowless and silent except for the faint noise of the lights.

He knew that his continued sojourn in this town was to some extent imposed by himself. It would have been easy for him to have bought a railway ticket and to have taken the train. Equally, he knew that such an action would have been hasty and somehow ill-advised. As he stood in the chapel he was relieved that he had shown circumspection. The quiet emptiness allowed him to examine his thoughts.

He no longer looked at the picture. It had been impossible to look at with detachment; he had seen in its ambiguity something which had had a direct relevance to himself. While he had looked at it again he had known that he had magnified its importance; its remote darkness surely had little to do with the present.

He stood in the body of the church.

A woman entered by a small door in the north transept. The door was set back and was half in shade; it was covered by an arras of faded green velvet. She looked round the church; the tin of metal-polish and the rags and yellow duster were brightly coloured things in her hands. She began to walk to the centre of the aisle.

'Do you know the time?' Alexander held up his hand to indicate that it was he who had spoken; his gesture was unnecessary for there were only the two of them in the church. The woman looked down the body of the church blankly, not seeing him.

'Excuse me. Do you know the time?' He began to walk towards her.

She shook her head. This simple gesture was familiar. Alexander recognized her as Mrs Killinger. Her headscarf and her coat had disguised her.

'Mrs Killinger.'

'Yes?' Then her searching eye saw him. 'It's you. I didn't see you at first.' She began to take off her coat. 'You must be a seasoned traveller to be able to find the places of interest so quickly.' She spoke in a loud conversational voice as though she were not in church; her voice was very much at variance with Alexander's, for even his shout had been muted and deferential.

'I didn't recognize you at first,' said Mrs Killinger. 'Your voice has altered. You sounded rather hoarse.'

72

She waited for him to catch up with her.

'You don't know the time?'

'Not exactly. I haven't got the watch with me; that's unusual. I often put my husband's watch in my pocket before I come out.' She looked at him as though he had changed since she had last seen him. 'Are you looking for anything in particular here?'

'I thought I might see the town.'

Mrs Killinger nodded silently as though he had said something profound. 'That's a good idea.' She smiled, suddenly, and her smile was unexpected. 'I hope everything's all right now.'

'What do you mean?'

'We heard you had an appointment to see someone on the first floor. I hope everything went well for you.'

'I think it did.'

'That's pleasing.' She glanced across to the other side of the church; perhaps she was reluctant to waste time. 'I ought to polish the lectern.' This seemed unnecessary; the lectern appeared to be highly burnished and the cold light blazed from its complex surfaces with brassy reflections.

'Do you know where I could find something to eat?'

'Certainly I do.' She turned back to him. 'It'll be impossible to give you your board in the house at present. When you are an official guest then that will be different. The inn near the railway does good food. Our lodger has his evening meal there. I give him his breakfast, but we can't give him dinner. My husband works shifts, you see, so I can't alter things to suit my lodger. One has to make arrangements according to one's circumstances, and unless I thought I could give him a certain guarantee I couldn't undertake to provide evening meals.' She came back to the point of her talk. 'I think you could do worse than at the inn.'

'That's helpful. Do you think they would give me a bed for the night?'

Mrs Killinger had turned away. Alexander had thought that her eyes had been following a living thing until he saw that her gaze rested upon a brass candle-holder which stood on the reading desk in front of the deacon's stall.

'Do they have accommodation at the inn?'

'I don't think so; not now. They used to, three or four years ago when it really was an inn. Now it seems it's too much trouble. You can see that by looking at the state of the place.'

'Can you suggest anywhere for me to spend the night?'

'I must think about that. There is a hotel but that would be expensive.'

'I don't know whether I have . . .'

'I was just wondering whether there was an empty servant's room which you might occupy. It would be unofficial, of course, and unofficial arrangements don't always work out for the best. A lot of the disused servants' rooms are used for storage, I think, but we might find somewhere to lay a mattress. It won't be much but at least you'd have a roof over your head.' She began to walk towards the lectern. 'We'll make those arrangements tomorrow; it's too late now. Tonight you could do worse than to ask Robert if you might sleep on the floor of his room. He might allow it for a consideration.'

Alexander had been staring round the church. It was unlike any church he had ever been in. 'Do you do a lot of work here?'

'Yes; increasingly so,' said Mrs Killinger with a smile. Her attitude was one of homely and good-natured pride. 'We all try to do what we can. There's a lot of cleaning and polishing to be done,' she said, though the stark interior of the church seemed to contradict her. 'Did you see the rota in the porch?'

'I didn't notice it.'

'Well, if you happen to look as you go out you'll find my name on it.'

Alexander pointed to the side chapel. 'Have you looked at that picture in there?' he asked.

Mrs Killinger seemed to be pleased that he had noticed it. 'Yes. It's a magnificent thing, isn't it? It's

74

wonderful to imagine how it has managed to hang together all these years. It's a curious old thing, isn't it? I've often looked at it. It's very dusty; I find it difficult to make out what's been painted. Sometimes I wonder why it's in the church; sometimes I wonder whether it's religious at all.'

'Perhaps the church ought to have it cleaned. As you say, it's very dusty.'

Mrs Killinger looked at Alexander as though she found his suggestion novel and unexpected. 'Have it cleaned? Who but you would have thought of that!' She shook her head, a gesture of mild surprise rather than of negativity. 'It's a very good idea. I don't think there is a restorer in the town and I am sure that the church would be reluctant to have it sent away. Perhaps they don't want it cleaned.'

'It's possible that it'll reach its full significance as an object of veneration only when it is pitch-black all over,' said Alexander sarcastically. He thought this might amuse Mrs Killinger.

'That's very possible,' she said, seriously. 'You know what you are talking about; you have a very apt way of putting things. What did you think of the other pictures?'

'There are other paintings?'

'Of course there are!' She laughed at his lack of observation. 'There's one on the west wall but it's hidden by the choir's cassocks. And then there are the pictures in the chancel.' She looked at him; she seemed to be still musing his suggestion that the picture might be cleaned. 'You ought to see the ones in the chancel.'

'You seem to find them important.'

'No, not really. I have to admit that I haven't looked at them closely; that's an odd fact. I suppose I've always had too much to do. I've heard other people talking about them, particularly the ones in the chancel. I overheard one visitor say that he thought it a pity that those pictures were so neglected. I expect he was right; they are misused. One of them hangs on the wall by the organ, and there is a nail in its frame so that the organist can hang his coat. The other one's used as a board where the numbers of the psalms are hung.'

Alexander felt an immediate desire to examine these two paintings. He walked up the aisle, following Mrs Killinger's pointing finger. She stood silently watching him as he passed through the chancel arch.

One of the paintings hung on the wall. It was almost hidden by the square cards of the psalm numerals. Alexander had to stand on the wooden bench of a reading desk in order to take the hanging cards off their hooks. It had been painted on a wooden board which had become cracked and warped with age. Twelve hooks had been screwed into its surface in order to hang the numerals. There was little left of the painting itself. The lower two thirds had long since gone, leaving only a stained and ochre-coloured gesso. The remaining third was relatively intact. A stylized pair of eyes was portrayed; they were about life size and they stared straight ahead. They were unmistakably male eyes. One of them had happened to be in the way when the painting had been made into a psalm board; a hook penetrated the pupil of the left eye. Apart from the eyes the painting was fragmentary. The two eyes, one injured and one staring, were by themselves beyond interpretation.

The other painting hung by the organ case as Mrs Killinger had said. It showed a man standing on a stone floor but with one foot resting on a low stool. He was bending over as though doing something to his foot; perhaps removing a thorn, or even doing something as mundane as tying a shoelace. The curious thing about the painting was that the man and the stool were tucked up into a corner of the painting, subordinate to the main subject of the picture. There was, however, no main subject; the painted surface had been abraded by some repetitive action, perhaps the hanging of a coat from the nail which had been driven into the top of the frame. The nail itself was bright and worn with long use. It had obviously been there for so many generations that the main subject of the picture must long ago have been lost to memory.

Alexander turned back to Mrs Killinger. 'What do you think they mean?' He began to walk back to rejoin her.

'I don't know. As I said, I've never really looked at them. I was only telling you the things I had heard. They are certainly old.'

'Yes, but that by itself means nothing. Who said that it was a pity that they had been neglected?'

'Only a visitor to the house. I'm not sure whether he was in conversation when he made that particular remark; he wasn't talking to me; I don't think he knew that I was in church. My memory may be faulty, but I'm sure he was exclaiming to himself.'

Mrs Killinger knelt at the foot of the lectern. She leaned forward to huff on the brasswork. Her breath clouded the metal; she began her unhurried polishing. The metal polish was unused. Her method of polishing was laborious and old-fashioned.

Alexander moved away from her and began to walk round the church again. He stood before the communion rail and looked back. Mrs Killinger was absorbed in her work. She knelt as though in prayer. There was a slow rhythm in the strokes of her polishing and her whole body moved backwards and forwards.

'How long have you been doing this?'

'This polishing? The brass rota?' She did not look up and there was no hesitation in her pace. 'I've been doing this for fifteen years. I started it when my father died.' Her voice was soft and withdrawn. 'He used to polish the brass; it was considered men's work then. He kept a baize apron especially for church work.'

'I didn't know the men used to do the polishing.'

'Things were different. The women were only welcome in the church at service-time. Father used to do the flagons and the dishes. The flowers are a new thing; you'd never see flowers on the altar in his day.'

Alexander had been aware of his growing hunger for some time. 'Mrs Killinger.'

'Yes?'

'I'm grateful for your help. It's been a long day for me.'

Mrs Killinger stopped her polishing. She began to stand, clumsily arching her back. While she had been polishing she had seemed supple and even graceful; now her age was apparent and there was an awkwardness about her movement. As she straightened herself she gave a sudden transient wince of pain. 'That's kind.' She seemed slightly embarrassed. 'It's a pleasure to be able to do something for a thoughtful person.'

'You shouldn't have troubled to stand.' Alexander wondered how he had deserved her old-fashioned courtesy.

'Oh, well. The only thing which surprises me is that you didn't spend long in looking at the pictures in the chancel.'

'There wasn't much to see.'

'I'm surprised that you should say that. Some of our visitors find them very interesting. There was one man who used to be in here for an hour at a time just looking at one of the pictures. He used to stand where you stood, on the seat of the reading desk. He'd carefully take the psalm numbers down and he'd look at the picture. The strange thing was that he had no interest in the other one.'

Alexander was tempted to go back and look at the painting; perhaps he had missed something. It was possible that there were further paintings, more distant and nearer the altar, hidden by the woodwork of the stalls. He dismissed the idea; his hunger pressed him. 'I must go now,' he said to Mrs Killinger.

2

Alexander stood in the lifeless hall of the house. He had
the staring, unsmiling manner of a man who has had to
come to terms with something unexpected and unpleasant during an evening's heavy drinking.

He had taken dinner at the inn near the railway, and
afterwards he had spent the evening in sporadic conversation with other men in the bar. They were mostly travellers; the two talkative ones used this inn as a staging
post on their regular journeys, and all they wished to do
was to drink and to tell jokes and anecdotes. Neither of
them had heard of the house or the course and neither
had any interest in them. Alexander had been pleased of
their company; they had dispelled the growing notion
that the town itself was peculiarly related to the course
he should have been attending. It was clear, looking at
these travellers, that the town might have been one of a
hundred little provincial market towns. When the inn
closed for the night and service had stopped, Alexander
was unexpectedly included in the select company
invited into an inner room for after-hours drinking. He
was gratified by the invitation, even if it had more to do
with the drinks he had been buying rather than any
brilliance of his company. The front door was locked
and they were drawn by the arm and beckoned silently
along a passage to the inner room where the late-night
drinking was done; a room lit only by a glimmer of light
and with a dusty bar and a dying fire. The atmosphere
was different here; drink was bought and sold in near
silence and unseen draperies muffled any sound. One of

the travellers had fallen asleep sitting at a table; the other was discussing the sleeping man's failing fortunes as though he had made a study of them.

A door opened and someone entered. He walked quickly, casting about the room; he was looking for someone. No one spoke to him.

'Alexander!' The tall man grasped Alexander's arm.

'What do you think you're doing?' Alexander had lost most of his fear of the man, perhaps because of the alcohol. 'I'm not going back there.'

'My master has something urgent to tell you.'

'At this hour?' Alexander saw that the others in the room were staring at him; without realizing it he saw that he must have been shouting. 'Take your hand off me. Where do you think you are? You're making a deplorable scene and I won't be party to it.'

The servant looked at him with contempt. 'If you had any sense you would put down that drink and listen.'

'Why does he want to see me?'

'How should I know? Come on; I'm late enough already. I've been all over the town looking for you.'

Alexander looked at his expressionless face. 'I see I can do nothing else.'

Now, alone, he stood in the lifeless hall. He had no wish to climb up the silent staircase but he was too worried by the summons to disobey it. He climbed up against a strong downward draught of dusty air. Above him the stairwell was lit by a single hanging bulb so high up that it would have been an acrobat's feat to change it.

He walked across the landing and down the passage of cast-off belongings. At the far door he stopped and looked back; behind him, beyond the silhouettes of the stacked books and the angular cases, the thin light of the hanging bulb was reflected from the brown linoleum in a diffuse streak. Alexander was angry with himself and he looked down the corridor as though he had no intention of going further. He was angry with himself because he had followed the servant so meekly; he told himself

that his meekness was due to a wish to end the embar-
rassing scene, but that was not true. The truth was that
he was anxious as to the outcome of the peremptory
summons. He knocked at the door and was told to enter.

The room, like the church, was lit by fluorescent
tubes; the light was intense; brighter than the daylight
he remembered.

'I want to give you the letter.' The voice had an edge to
it; the old diffidence was gone. He held out the envelope.

'Did you call me here just for that?'

'Just for that? Who do you think you are?' He took a
sudden step forwards, towards Alexander, almost as if
he were going to attack him; he was checked in this in
very much the same way that a dog on a running-chain is
checked when the end of the chain is reached. He put a
hand to his neck and then to his head, running his long
fingers through his black hair. 'Have you no sense?' He
shouted as though he had been shocked into exclaiming
his unreasoned first thoughts. 'Do you know what this
letter means? Perhaps it was of little importance once;
who can say what its importance is now?' He lowered
his voice. 'The repairs are obvious, but they are the best
that could be done at the time.'

His manner made Alexander fearful. The concern of
the other man had been very real; even in his present
and controlled anxiety for Alexander his sincerity was
plain. 'What makes you think it has become so important?' asked Alexander.

The man spoke with a precise urgency as though his
words all carried an equal weight. 'You've lived a cautious life until now. You've always behaved with the
discretion which is so necessary for an existence among
circumstances which are changing as yours are. Why
waste all that you have undergone because of one
moment's irrational behaviour?' He held out the
envelope.

Alexander took it. He opened the letter and saw that
the page had been gummed together with edging paper
from a block of stamps. The repair had been crudely

carried out; Alexander could have made a far better job of it himself. For some reason the inexpert roughness of the repair added to his anxiety. 'I may have been acting irrationally when I tore this, but I don't see how it has become more important now.'

'Haven't I told you the answer to that? How could I have spoken more plainly? I told you about those who had been disadvantaged because they had lost the written proof of their summons. I told you about those who started off with a disadvantage because their summons had been by telephone. If you remember, you tore the letter within a few minutes of me telling you of your good fortune in having an intact letter.'

'I meant what I did.'

'I don't believe you. You acted on impulse and you were impelled by childish irritation.' He stopped talking. It was easy to see that he had been speaking out of concern for Alexander.

'You seem to mean what you say,' said Alexander.

'I'm in no position of authority,' he continued. 'When you first came I told you that anything I said had no official authority; I said that I had met no-one who had ever found the official course of instruction; I said that I had over the years been able to give, for want of better words, a "course of instruction" to those who came in answer to a summons. Implicit in that course – if you can call it a course – is its unofficial nature. I have received no official sanction and no official communication or comment has been sent to me. I think I even told you that I thought perhaps you had found me too quickly and too easily; it seemed to me that you were going into things too quickly to appreciate them; too quickly to sort out the valuable from the worthless: you appeared to be glossing over the meaning of things. Here I am, offering you a letter which has been repaired. You still don't realize the importance of it.'

'How can I? What is it?'

'Why do you ask such questions? If you thought about it you'd know that I could give no direct answer. All I can do is to talk obliquely about things from my own experience. You'll have to believe your letter to be important without proof.

'I know that it was initially of little importance. It seems to be quite clear that if you had torn it up nothing would have happened. But you did not tear it up then; you chose to follow it, earnestly at first but then with a dilatory amateurishness when the going became difficult. By starting to follow its instructions you have committed yourself to it. You could have laughed at it once but you can't do that now.'

'I have to believe you. You look serious enough.'

'I ought to be honest with myself; you are very new here.' He paused and glanced at the letter. 'It's a bad repair. I didn't have time to do it myself and you can't pick and choose who does these tasks for you.

'I'll tell you what I know. When you first gave me that letter to read I saw that it had been well-fingered. This showed that you had carried it about with you and that you constantly referred to it in the short time you had had it. This surprised me, because the message is brief, and there is hardly anything to refer to. Why had this bald letter worried you? I had already begun to form an opinion of you from your treatment of the letter. I had seen the slight creases in it, as though it had been passed from hand to hand, or as though two people had been looking at it together. This meant that you had shown it to other people; you were so concerned about the message that you wished other opinions on its meaning. Incidentally, I should avoid showing it to other people in the future. These letters are private, and they say that it is possible to take advantage of someone by reading his letter.

'Now it's torn.' He looked at Alexander, and, as if aware that there was a speciousness in what he was saying, he smiled slightly. 'Perhaps you think I'm being unreasonable in my insistence on the importance of the letter. Judged by one standard it is only a piece of paper. Judged by another it has a very different meaning.' He shrugged his shoulders. 'Many men and women come up here and show their letters to me. I know too well their watchful mannerisms, their raised hands; they are eager for me to read but unable to allow the pages out of their sight. One doesn't know what to do, at first; it takes some getting used to. The page is often thrust into one's face but the sides are held tightly. The eyes stare; there is no expression but watchfulness in the face, lest I might be no more than a conjuror who, by subtle movements of the hand, might cheat them of their guide and perhaps substitute something almost identical but robbed of worth and that almost magical importance with which these letters are imbued!

'Now you can see why I stress the importance of that letter. It is difficult for me to stress it as fully as I ought because I have become so used to the anxieties of my visitors. When I first took my post here I made it my duty to attempt to show an empathy. This proved to be an impossibility, and yet at the time it seemed that nothing else was enough. Later, the exhibition of the letters became mundane. I found I had to put on a false expression of interest and concern. I was being given letters to read so often that I could hardly be bothered with them. Vague typed sentences, hinting at things I did not understand, valued for reasons which seemed to be wrong. The recipients stared at me, and when questioned, could do no more than express those old inarticulate anxieties which I was beginning to know so well.'

'Perhaps you're saying that your concern was false.'

He looked at Alexander. 'I don't think so. I'm telling the truth of my own experiences to you because you might benefit from them. You haven't begun to deceive yourself over the importance of the letter you received. I'm speaking to you honestly; at the moment I would find difficulty in doing otherwise.

'There is,' he said, 'a trade in the forgery of these letters. It is possible for those who have lost their letters to go to one of at least a dozen businessmen – I know them all by repute – to dictate letters, perhaps as they

84

think they received them, perhaps as they think they ought to have received them. Most of these attempts would be very amateurish, had not the scribes been skilful. The reproductions are still faulty; the maxim has gone round: "the signature is difficult to remember", and all the while the text has been altered by an omission of factual detail or an inclusion of fallacious material; superimposed on this are the scribes' mannerisms and idiosyncrasies. But all this is tangential to the thing I am trying to warn you against. I want to ask you a question.'

'I'm willing to listen.'

'And willing to answer, I hope. I want you to tell me your first impression when you first saw your letter.'

'It arrived at my lodgings and I opened it in the dining room.'

'No; what was your first impression of it?'

'What do you mean? When I first looked down at the unopened envelope?'

'Yes, that is what I mean. What was your first impression?'

'The fact that the stationery was unusual made me more than ordinarily observant. As I took hold of it and reached for the knife I knew that my anxiety was foolish. Another moment, the envelope open, and I would have in my hands a government circular, the agenda of a committee, a communication about tax. Nothing more. But I opened the envelope, and the sheet of paper inside seemed so exactly to accord with what I had expected (but not admitted even to myself) that I was astonished. Then the moment passed, and I put it down to *déjà vu*, or a trick of memory. I had been hardly awake for more than a few minutes.' He held the letter in his hands, feeling the joins in the crudely-mended sheet. The room was too bright for comfort; the long fluorescent lamps allowed no shadows.

'Do you see,' said the other man, 'that the phrasing of the words may mislead you as to the meaning of the letter?' He saw Alexander's scepticism. 'Yes, you're well fed now. You feel at ease. It's a very superficial feeling. I suppose you can't think ahead to the time when you'll have an empty stomach.' He had raised his voice. 'What have you achieved at the moment? How will you achieve anything if you approach the change in your circumstances in your present manner? You might as well realize that there is no possibility of turning back now; everything you will undergo has its origins in something self-imposed and in the past. You say that you don't understand the importance of the letter, yet you conformed willingly to its most minute instruction, truncating your past life with barely a thought.'

'I think it might have been the same had the letter never arrived.' He looked down at his letter.

'Look at your letter if you like. What will you do tonight? Where will you find a room? What will you do tomorrow night?'

Alexander saw that the standing man himself looked tired; indeed, he seemed rather more tired than Alexander. His voice sounded exhausted and dull.

'I'll sleep anywhere,' said Alexander.

'I don't doubt it. There's the complacency of meat and alcohol in your very manner.' He had taken a pace backwards so that he leaned against the back of the chair. He looked past Alexander at the door. 'You're an over-conditioned creature or you wouldn't have listened to me for so long and at such a time.' He shook his head; perhaps he had not expressed his thoughts as he had intended. 'What's the time?'

'How should I know?'

'I saw you look at your wrist.'

Alexander looked at his wrist again, aware for the first time that he had forgotten his watch. 'It's habit. I must have taken my watch off.' He turned and walked halfway to the door.

The other man's voice made him stop. 'I've not said anything to try to impress you. I know this house well and yet I've been forced to answer your questions in a vague manner. Perhaps it's my experience which makes me circumlocutory and indecisive. I'm aware that I've contradicted myself. A tyro, standing where I stand, might have been more help to you; he would have helped you to select the invented rule which best suited your immediate purpose. He would have stated a definite opinion, even though it might be the opinion of the last teacher he remembered, and not his own. The novice makes himself the mouthpiece of the fashionable pedagogue heard last.' He looked away. 'I talk too much. I'm too much of a novice myself to have any authority to speak.'

Alexander stood by the door and turned the handle. 'What do you want from me?'

'What do I want? Have you misunderstood me so utterly?'

Alexander opened the door and stood in the corridor outside. A sudden wind blew down the long passage, singing under the doors hidden by the heaps of lumber. The door of the room behind him slammed shut. The brilliance vanished, and the corridor was, by contrast, black and lightless.

He hesitated at the door, his eyes unadapted to the darkness. He put out a hand to feel his way and touched a pile of stacked papers. He withdrew his hand with a jerk. He had not been sure what he touched; for a second it seemed that he had touched a face. The papers fell to the floor with a continued slithering sound. He saw nothing but phosphenes and the images of the long lights of the room behind him.

His senses told him that he was not alone in the passage. A few yards away, in the dim light which filtered down from the high panes at the top of the light shaft, he saw a face which was as moveless as a mask and as grainy and indistinct as a face in an old photograph.

Several of the staff stood in the corridor, unmoving, standing in the niches between the stacked crates and chests. In the vague light he could make nothing of their faces; each one was blank and half-imagined, but he saw in each face a blank intensity. It was easy, in a flight of imagination, to imagine that they waited for some prearranged signal; at its sounding they would jump from their hiding-places and, at the sounding of another signal, would pinion him and lead him away to an unknown room deep in the bulk of the house.

Someone turned the light on at the end of the passage. The servants blinked in the light. Any intensity of expression must have been imagined; most of them looked half asleep. They had made themselves comfortable while they waited; a few of them sat on the stacked packing-cases, their heads near the ceiling, their faces owlish. One man, leaning against the wall, yawned and by reflex put up his hand to his mouth, the first action which any of them had taken. Further down the corridor two women stood together, their twin expressions registering nothing but a tired boredom; they looked as though they had been talking together but had been interrupted by the opening of the door.

Alexander stood with his back to the door and faced the cluttered passageway.

'He's tired. Of course he's tired.' The voice was flat and without expression; an old woman had spoken. She stood in the shadows and it was difficult to see her face clearly.

This statement, given out as though Alexander had been deaf or inanimate, made him angry. 'I'm not tired. If I were, what difference would it make to you?'

The old woman shook her head. She looked up at another of the servants, a young woman. 'You see, I told you. He's very tired.'

Alexander began to walk down the corridor. As he walked he passed the old woman and he muttered, 'Yes, he's tired. Not that it matters one way or the other to you. But it doesn't do any good,' and he stared at her as he passed, 'to keep on saying, "He's tired!" ' He had used a tone of exaggerated mimicry while repeating the phrase; the female servant whom the old woman had been addressing giggled, and the old woman herself blushed and turned away.

'You shouldn't have done that,' someone else whispered, his face sidelong to Alexander's. 'She has your welfare at heart; that's why she spoke. Friends should be welcome, particularly to someone like yourself.' He put out a forefinger. 'You ought to find out more about people before you decide to snap at them.'

This did nothing more than to irritate Alexander, though it irritated him more than he might have thought possible. 'You can keep quiet for a start,' he said.

'What's the matter?' The voice was very earnest. The speaker looked at the door through which Alexander had come. 'Has Mr Turnbull given you a hard time?'

'Mr Turnbull?' Alexander looked back at the closed door. 'Is that his name?'

'We call him Mr Turnbull, though that was the name of his predecessor. This one's more reticent; he hasn't bothered to tell us his name.' He paused as though aware of a lie which might later be discovered. 'He did tell us his name, but he's still called by the name of his predecessor. There's no reason for that, except that it's a government-run apartment, and it is let to a man called Turnbull. Mr Turnbull, you might say, assumed the tenancy of the room and the name at the same time.' He looked at Alexander as though this statement might not be enough. 'It was,' he continued, 'far more logical to keep the old name than to adjust the precedents and alter the various documents which govern the tenure and the status of his position accordingly.'

'Was he happy to assume the name of his predecessor?' Alexander asked the question, though it was clear that he had asked it out of a tired formality; he had no wish to know the answer. He rested against a pile of boxes. He closed his eyes. He rested himself in an attitude of drowsy anger.

'He is tired.'

'Of course he doesn't mind changing his name,' said the man, drowning the old woman's voice. 'At least, not officially. The old name identifies him in his post. His name is a title in itself, and does away with the need for the invocation of titles.' He drew the long fingers of his right hand through his hair. 'I don't suppose you know that you have achieved a variety of names since you first came here. I don't suppose you know even that.'

'I didn't,' said Alexander.

'Well . . .' The servant paused; he cocked his head to one side, examining Alexander, who had closed his eyes as though he slept. 'You look too tired to be interested.'

'I am tired,' said Alexander. 'She's right.' He opened his eyes and looked at the servants collectively, as though he saw them for a moment as being part of the same organism. 'Where can I sleep?'

'I told you he was tired.'

'Be quiet.' Alexander half turned; for a moment all trace of sleep left his face.

'What's up with you?' A fresh voice spoke. Alexander recognized it as being Mrs Killinger's. 'You're acting entirely out of character!'

'What's up with me? Did you mean to ask that? What's up with this house: that's the question which needs an answer!'

'Do you want a room for the night?'

'Yes, I do.'

'Well, then, you can be plain about it.' Mrs Killinger stood in the middle of the passage. She smiled her usual cultured smile and her face showed an enigmatic compassion. 'There's a bed of sorts prepared for you. That's why I came up here. You ought to have recognized that. I've waited for some time.'

'What are the rest of them doing here?' He wondered how long they had been standing in the dark. He looked at them; they shuffled about uncomfortably when they saw themselves observed.

'Perhaps you would care to follow Mrs Farrard. She'll show you to the place you've been given.'

Mrs Farrard was the old woman who had repeatedly insisted that Alexander was tired; now she stood by herself, rebuffed and ill at ease, her head sunk into her shoulders. In other circumstances she might have been crying; there was a complete lack of resilience about her. Alexander realized that his mimicry of her stock phrase had embarrassed her far more than was reasonable.

She began to walk down the corridor, expecting Alexander to follow; she did not turn to Alexander and she ignored the other servants as though she felt herself to be humiliated.

When they were on the landing Alexander called to her. 'Excuse me for a minute.'

She stopped; the rapid sound of her pattering feet echoed in the silence of the stairwell. In the light of the high bulb, small and remote though it was, her face had a mushroom-coloured tint. Below her eyes two damp vertical lines formed runnels in the powder.

They walked down the stairs. Mrs Farrard, hesitant at every step and clasping the rail and feeling ahead with her other hand as though it were dark, seemed exhausted by the time she stood in the hall. She looked at the sea of slippery brown linoleum as though afraid to venture out on it; she still had one hand stretched out in front of her as if she were unsure of her balance. Her paces were tiny and shuffling. When Alexander offered his support she gladly took his arm. She directed their way across the hall. They were alone.

'I'm sorry if I behaved badly,' said Mrs Farrard. 'And thank you for helping me. I'm old now and I want to hold on to things when I walk. I should hate to fall; they make no concessions to the elderly. It's easy to break a hip if you fall awkwardly.' She said these things in an under-tone; perhaps she did not mean to speak them aloud. She suddenly looked up at him. Alexander realized how tiny she was. 'I'm sorry if I behaved badly,' she said again. 'It's just that I never know the right thing to say in front of them. They can be so scathing if you say the wrong thing and they keep on bringing the subject up at meal times.' Her voice hardly raised an echo from the glossy walls. 'They can never leave the subject alone,' she said,

91

mechanically, as though rapid speech might help her preserve her balance. 'It's difficult for a highly-strung person like me to have to live here, in the servants' hall, amid all the gossip.'

'They gossip, do they?' Alexander had spoken merely to put the old woman at ease, but as he spoke he felt her nervous grip tighten on his arm. Perhaps she was afraid that they might be overheard; perhaps she just had difficulty in keeping her balance.

'My word, you're right!' The diminutive face stared briefly up at Alexander, almost gratefully, as if the old woman was not used to hearing anything which confirmed her own statements. 'They do gossip. I said something once when I was new here, years ago – they said I was pretty, where I came from, though of course I shouldn't be forward enough to venture whether it was true or not; I was young then – I said something: one word. One word in reply to something an old servant had said. It was at lunch, in the servants' hall. I felt so lonely, so I spoke. Apparently it had not been the right thing to say.' She shook her head. 'They remembered that. It became my nickname. They would say that word to one another, and they would titter behind their hands. They used to enjoy laughing at my expense because I didn't have their . . .' She paused to search for a word, did not find one, and gave the sentence up. 'It was like that tonight while we were waiting for you. They don't change; their character is just the same, even if the generations move on. That's all beside the point. Mrs Killinger said that you were in Mr Turnbull's room and that you wanted a bed. Someone was sent off to put a mattress on the floor of Robert's room. They seem to use that room a lot for occasional visitors who haven't been accepted into the house yet, such as yourself . . .'

'So I shall have to sleep in Robert's room,' said Alexander resignedly.

'It's better than nowhere. But that's by the way.' Mrs Farrard gripped Alexander's arm, tightly, her volubility not diminishing her fear of falling. 'So I was sent up to

Mr Turnbull's room to wait outside his door. Mrs Killinger came up with me, and a few of the other servants, too. They tend to get bored in the evenings, and that makes them inquisitive. We saw you come up the stairs and knock at his door.'

'I never saw you standing there when I arrived.'

'Perhaps you wouldn't have done. No one bothered to switch on the light. Mr Apsleigh's assistant heard you coming and whispered for us to be silent. He is very inquisitive. I am not like that; my country upbringing makes me mind my own business. I usually try to keep out of the way when we have visitors like yourself. But what I was going to say was that I had never seen you before. You had been described to me, of course; the rest of them had been watching you. I knew what you would look like – Mr Apsleigh's assistant is very good at describing people who come into the house – and when I saw you for the first time I was struck by your weariness. I only saw you for an instant; for a second while you opened the door and the light streamed out. I heard you talking to Mr Turnbull. I wondered why he was so thoughtless in keeping you for so long when you looked so tired. Mr Apsleigh's assistant whispered that he could smell drink when you stumbled past, though I thought you were stumbling because of the clutter in the passage.'

'Mr Turnbull was, I think, only trying to help me.'

'Perhaps so. That's by the way. When I saw you I said to myself, "He's tired". I only wanted to say what I felt.' She was near to tears; Alexander could hear the catch in her voice. They were in a stretch of corridor unfamiliar to him. A wall-lamp showed Mrs Farrard's glistening eyes. 'I always come out with the wrong words,' she said. 'They'll be talking about that for a long time in the servants' hall. Particularly Giles. He's always looking for an example of other people's mistakes, and he's unrelenting. He's observant and he's a horrible mimic. He was doing his mimicry of you when we were at dinner, as though he had some point to make. He's a clever

93

man. "You can use him as an illustration," he said. "Look at him when he first comes here, anxious for the fulfilment of his ambitions, whatever they are. Look at him when he sees that his ambitions are misdirected. Look at him . . ." he looked round the servants' hall as we stared up at him ". . . when he realizes that he has to come down to you." He made fun of us by his mimicry of you. "Who is forced to stay here?" he said. He flies in the face of convention; I sometimes think he isn't worthy of an official position . . .'

'All right,' said Alexander, interrupting the old woman. 'I haven't met this Giles, but he'll remember me if I catch him at it.'

'That's not the point,' said Mrs Farrard impatiently. Alexander was beginning to realize that she had not listened to a single thing he had said. 'That's not the point at all. The truth is that you can't keep a single thing secret here. I remember when I came from the country; when I first came. That would be many years ago. The only thing I brought with me was a wooden box.' She was on the verge of weeping. 'It was only a wooden box, I suppose, but it was important to me because my father had made it especially for my journey. It's a forlorn and stupid memory I know, but I can see him now as he made that box. He was good with his hands. I remember watching him work, at home in the village. He was a good carpenter. It seems foolish to divulge these things to you because they aren't important, but I can remember his hands, at the same time so capable and so loving.'

'He made you a wooden box,' said Alexander.

'I think he made it me because he knew I was going away and because he knew that I would want something which he had made with his own hands. It was only a box, but it was my pride while I travelled. When I was faced with the official forms and the difficulties of changing trains and the interviews with the officials I could always console myself by touching the corners of that box and feeling the dovetails of the joints with my fingers.' She began to cry, unable to speak, though her lips still moved.

Alexander was at a loss to know how to comfort her. 'Did you come here as a maid?' He felt the tremulousness of her arm in the crook of his own.

'No. When I came here it wasn't like that.' The recollection brought a fresh burst of tears. Her face was wet.

'Why did you come here?' Alexander's voice was soft and solicitous.

'They sent a letter to me. It arrived at my father's house. Times were difficult; no-one could spare a moment. The fact that I had received a letter made me important. I had been taught only simple language, and its meaning was beyond my understanding. I took it secretly to our priest.'

'What did it say?' Alexander felt the familiarity of his own anxiety. 'Can you remember that?'

Mrs Farrard stopped crying and she looked up from her reminiscences. Her manner was set with suspicion. 'It was a very private letter.'

'I'm sorry. I only wanted to help you. Perhaps your letter was like mine.'

'Oh, yes, that's what they all say when they want something; "show me your letter; it may be like mine", they say; you can't trust them. I found that when I first came here. That private letter was in the box which my father had made; it didn't take them long to force the lock of the box when they knew that I had been sent away down to the guests' wing to clean the hearths. The letter was gone from the lining of the box. I swore that I would remember that mean act.' She disengaged her arm from Alexander's, and began to walk down the corridor on her own, feeling for the painted wall. 'I was beginning to take a liking to you; I can't help it; I want to do the best for people. My heart went out to you when I saw you at the door of Mr Turnbull's room; I thought your weariness was genuine. I never learn. I suppose I ought to talk less.' Her voice was abrupt, as though she spoke each thought as it came into her mind. 'Now if you don't mind I think we'll go directly to the yard where I can direct you to Robert's room.' She beckoned for Alexander to follow her; an unnecessary gesture, for he was close behind her. She shot him an irritated glance. She was silent as she led the way forward; had she not spoken as she had, Alexander would have been forced to recognize an attitude of prior commitment, as though this errand was delaying her and keeping her from carrying out a more important task.

The door which led to the courtyard was unexpected. It had clearly been fairly recently inserted into the corridor; the brickwork surrounding it was unplastered. The door was narrow and metal-framed; the glass was a heavy modern safety-glass with a mesh of wire. It appeared to be well used; the handle and the metal footrail were polished by the constant passage of people. Mrs Farrard opened the door, looking down as she stepped out into the courtyard. Her lips were pursed as she carefully negotiated the uneven flagstones. Alexander followed her.

The courtyard was unexpected. Hitherto the house had shown itself to be a building of no great size; now it seemed that that first impression had been mistaken. The courtyard behind the house, facing the hill, instead of giving onto the moorland slopes of the hill was bounded by wooden buildings which stood three or four storeys high. There was no order to them, as though temporary construction had followed temporary construction. It was, on further examination, difficult to tell how tall they were; the hillside was steep. The frontages of the wooden buildings stretched away. There were a number of doors which led out onto the uneven courtyard, though the only door into the older part of the house seemed to be the metal-framed door through which they had passed. Looking at the wooden buildings again it was apparent that they were not as recent as they had appeared. Much of the wooden cladding, unpainted, was rotting and much of the corrugated iron had rusted through. There was a dank smell of bitumen and old creosote in the air.

Mrs Farrard stood at the bottom of a wooden staircase, narrow but ascending steeply. The door was kept open by a hook and a cloud of insects had gathered on the plasterboard of the ceiling in the light of the lamp. 'Up at the top of this you'll find his room.'

'I see.'

'Well, I hope you have a good night.' Mrs Farrard behaved as though she were not quite familiar with this place. She put a hand to her face. 'I'm sorry for you. I wish I could help you.'

There was something so ineffectual and powerless about the way she said this that Alexander was forced to laugh. 'Why should you wish to help me?'

'Because you looked so tired, there, outside that room.'

Alexander looked up at the staircase ahead of him. 'Is that a reason?'

'Yes, it is. I don't think you're as strong as you think you are,' she suddenly exclaimed. 'Besides, even if that wasn't so, your tiredness has you defeated before you can start. You're a newcomer here, but I understand you better than you think. I see that you face things bravely. Don't forget that I come from the country; I am very observant. You face things bravely, not allowing yourself to express any surprise. You even look up at these rotting buildings which lie behind the noble facade of the house as though you expected to find them here. All because you have a confidence in yourself.' She stood next to Alexander; her voice was secretive as though she were voicing her own thoughts aloud rather than speaking to him. 'I suppose we all have a kind of unreasonable confidence in ourselves when we first come here. It isn't so much a fault as a misunderstanding.' She looked at him. 'You won't be comfortable up there.'

Alexander looked at her, his manner indulgent. 'I don't mind doing without comfort.'

'It's not that. You have self-confidence. You think, at the moment, that this is all a transient thing. Tomorrow

97

it'll be gone; tomorrow you'll be able to go back to your city; tomorrow you'll be away, laughing perhaps. I have seen it all before. I have been through it. I have seen them staring up from that courtyard, looking at these wooden buildings as though they were doing nothing more than storing up anecdotes for future telling. It isn't like that.'

'If you wish me to be honest I would say that you weren't making much sense.'

'That's because you haven't experienced it yet.'

'Experienced what?' Alexander was thinking back to the time when the old woman had been overcome by a flood of tears at the memory of the wooden box her father had made.

'Well, at the moment you think you're self-sufficient. It never works like that. Often those with the greatest confidence in themselves come off badly. It begs the question as to why they have so much confidence in themselves. I'm not sure. You'll find the need for good advice. All our heads are defenceless.'

'I need good advice at the moment.'

'That's a good sign. The first thing one has to do is to find a source of it.'

'I'm very tired.'

This statement, baldly given, was enough to make the old woman bow her head. She left the bottom of the stair. Her irregular and hesitant footsteps retreated across the courtyard. A moment later there was a metallic noise as the narrow door to the corridor was shut.

Alexander began to climb the stairs.

A wind was up, and, seen through an open landing window, a furrowed cloud field obscured the stars. The falling of a light summer rain was imminent.

Alexander climbed the stairs. As he climbed he saw the temporary nature of the building he was now in. The place was built to the lowest building standards, though it was not possible to determine immediately whether this had been done to save time or cost or, possibly, both.

The lower stairs were of rough concrete, unfinished, as though the shuttering used in their construction had just been removed. The walls and ceiling were of painted fibreboard and batten.

Despite the austere parsimony of the building it was very familiar to Alexander. The stamp of contemporary government construction was inherent in everything that surrounded him. When he came to the top of the stairs he saw the narrow landing and the standard doors of thin timber and plywood. Beyond each door might have been an office. Instead, three of the doors were locked with inappropriate outdoor padlocks and their handles and the strips of linoleum before their thresholds were dusty with disuse. He knocked at the panels of the fourth door. There was no reply.

He opened the door and turned on the light. The room was slightly larger than he had expected, and its shape was somewhat different; it was odd in retrospect, but he had had the dimensions of the room mapped out in his mind's eye while he had still been standing on the landing and before he had opened the door. It was not quite the room he expected. He looked about him.

The panelled walls were distempered with a green paint which had discoloured with time. The ceiling, made of bulging fibreboards between strips of wood, was painted white. In one corner, distant from the hanging light, the roof had leaked and the walls and ceiling were mildewed. Underneath the window stood an iron bedstead, the bedding unmade. Along a wall a mattress had been placed; on it there were a couple of grey blankets, loosely folded. Alexander assumed that he was to sleep on the mattress. Accordingly he removed his shoes, his jacket and tie, and placed these garments against the wall. He walked to the door and turned off the light, and, standing still to allow himself to become accustomed to the pale light of the infiltrating moon, he looked again at the configuration of the room. He lay down on the mattress and pulled the blankets about him, reaching out for his jacket and using it as a pillow.

His mind had been busy with the constant change which had happened since the arrival of the letter. In fact, he knew that he had deliberately allowed his mind to become pre-occupied with a study of his surroundings. His environment could at least be observed in a neutral light. He knew as he lay, staring up at the ceiling, that he had done his best to prevent himself from analysing his own thoughts and the impressions of the things he had seen. Alone, now, he feared introspection.

He had come here in answer to a letter and had found nothing but uncertainty. He had no ally. He had found no clue that might help him. He had found nobody whose judgement he could trust. The point of the letter had never been anything but vague; now it was shifting and diffuse but there could still be no doubt about its importance. For some reason the incoherence of the day's events emphasized that importance until it was uppermost in his mind. It was difficult to be rational about what had taken place. Only a disordered sequence of the day's events came back to him.

He recalled, almost without conscious will, various phrases that he had heard. At the time of hearing they had been only phrases; now they had taken on an indefinable significance. He remembered, with an unusual clarity of memory, Mr Turnbull's words: 'You've lived your life in a cautious and circumspect manner until now. Why waste all your efforts because of a single moment's irrationality?' He knew that his recall had been erroneous. The man had surely said: 'You've lived a cautious life until now. You've always behaved with the circumspection and the discretion necessary for an existence *in changing circumstances*. Why waste all that you have undergone?' Alexander was not sure whether Mr Turnbull had emphasized any of his words; perhaps the emphasis lay in Alexander's imagination. The fact that Mr Turnbull took it for granted that Alexander was living in changing circumstances did not make for any peace of mind. He was aware that this dwelling on minutiae was only a mechanism for escaping the sense of what Turnbull had said. He had spoken with an extreme urgency. Why had he shouted? What had been Alexander's irrational action? Had his obedience to the vague summons been irrational? Alexander recalled the manner in which the man had spoken: he had shouted involuntarily.

'I've acted in the manner I thought best.' As Alexander said this to himself he knew, or thought he did, the reason for his agitation when he had first seen the letter. The letter had not been, or so it appeared now, at all unexpected. Had he thought about it he could have predicted its arrival. Had he not been preoccupied with the routine of the day's work he would have found it an easy prediction.

Perhaps those who had received telephone messages could have predicted their summons in the same way. Alexander had a suspicion that the recipient of such a telephone call would be in an uneasy and troubled sleep before the telephone rang and the message arrived; in the half-light between sleep and wakefulness the bell would have rung in imagination before ever it sounded in reality.

Why now was the message so important? It had provoked an anxiety which had made the search for its origin a necessity. What other purpose could it serve?

'I have read too much into it,' he said, aloud, and the painted fibreboard of the walls and the ceiling absorbed the sound.

There was some comfort to be gained in thinking back to the time before the arrival of the letter. He thought about his work.

He had attended many meetings at the Brownian Institute. One day-long meeting came back to him vividly; he was not sure why this was; it had been in no way peculiar or out of the ordinary. This meeting (it had been called, somewhat euphemistically, a symposium) had occurred about eighteen months or two years ago. He had been pleased that he had been invited to attend that meeting. He had taken in the words of each speaker, given as they had been with the security of reputation and authority. He had heard the expression of the blinkered conciseness of generalization. Now he was aware of the deception and the rhetoric and the unimportance of accuracy in the statement of the well-worn arguments which led easily to the expected conclusions. He wondered how he could have listened to such arguments in such an unquestioning way.

He recalled a review paper by the last speaker at that meeting. It was a reprint from a journal, and he had found it lying on his colleague's bench. He had borrowed it and had read it in his lunch hour. He had thought it well written; he had long ago accepted the familiar choice of phrase, the idiosyncrasies of grammar so currently in vogue, the interweaving of unexplained neologisms and undefined definitions. He remembered the conclusions which rested on observations stated as being 'self-obvious' but which were not. The fact that the paper had been reprinted from a reputable journal made the reasoning impeccable. The impress of truth had been stamped upon it, and that in itself was a conclusion.

'I thought I could recognize a lie like that,' said Alexander.

His thoughts went out towards his colleague, the hardworking man with whom he shared his laboratory. At first Alexander had thought him slow and obstinate in his caution in picking up new ideas. He had thought him insular, quirky, willing to mask his ignorance in a cloak of dry but unembittered scepticism towards new thought. After a few months Alexander had begun to appreciate his other qualities; lately he had begun to appreciate that the 'new thought' was perhaps old work polished up with jargon and modern phraseology.

Alexander felt embarrassed at the tolerance his colleague had shown to his own rendition of his teachers' crystalline ideas and forceful and even stormy opinions. His colleague had remarked, mildly, more than once:

'One should state a finding no more than once; only a hack, not content with making a point, has to repeat it.' Occasionally he had grown humorously sarcastic: 'A lot of them bang their drums, and the skins get very thin. The trick is to know when to stop banging the drum before the skin ruptures.' He had raised his eyebrows. 'I can only admire your enthusiasm for them.'

Alexander must have fallen asleep though he was not aware of having done so. His train of thought was incomplete.

Someone had turned the light on; it seemed to be harsher than before. The person who had turned on the light was walking about the floor.

'Who are you?' The voice was feminine; despite the question it lacked any curiosity. 'The visitor, the one they were talking about, I suppose,' she said.

Alexander looked about him. The room seemed to have altered since he had fallen asleep. The light hung directly over his head and the conical white shade threw the brilliant glare downwards so that the rest of the room was grey and indefinable. 'The visitor?'

'Yes. Mrs Farrard was talking about you.'

'I suppose I am the visitor, then.'

'Couldn't they find you a more suitable place than this?'

He screwed up his eyes but could still see nothing beyond the light. He still felt himself to be asleep; the light, brilliant though it was, seemed to have a different cast of colour in its incandescence. It was possible that there might be truth in this; in the late night the voltage of the electricity supply may have increased as the demand grew less. 'I thought this was Robert's room.'

The voice hesitated before answering. 'Yes, it is.'

The light was turned off. Only the glow of the bedside light remained; this little steel lamp had not been apparent while the main light had been on.

Alexander looked at her; she sat on the edge of the bed. She was undoing the buttons of her blouse. He looked away. 'I'm sorry,' he said. 'They must have mis-directed me.'

'No. This is the room; I've just said that it's Robert's room. I'm used to other people in here.' She paused. Her voice took on a careless animation which might have been quite lively had she not seemed tired. 'I don't mind it any more. He likes to regard me as his woman; he's called me that before now, in company.'

She began to undress; it was impossible for Alexander not to look at her.

'I must go,' he said.

'No,' she said. 'You haven't been allocated anywhere else, have you? Besides, it's just as well to do what the servants tell you; they know a lot of things that we don't.'

'You aren't a servant, then?'

She paused in her undressing. 'No. I could never be a servant.' She smiled slightly. 'I suppose I am what I am; Robert's woman. There's no need not to be outspoken about it. I'm too tired to pretend to be modest; I've been through all that in the past.'

She was naked.

Alexander could hardly take his gaze from her. 'Are you expecting him to be here this evening?'

'I never know when to expect him.'

'You are too good for him,' he said, looking at her.

She climbed into bed, quickly, perhaps embarrassed at last. 'You don't know what you're saying.' Her voice had lost some of its tiredness. 'He's more important than you think; he knows what he's about in his own world.'

'You are too good for him,' said Alexander again. 'He's an extortioner. You're not like that; you're far more intelligent than he is. You're an attractive girl in a strange place that can mean nothing to you. What are you doing here? You shouldn't be like this . . . I can see that you're stuck in something which can be no more than a routine. Robert's a servant with a servant's mind; he's an extortioner.'

'What did he do to make you think that?'

'It's of no importance now. You can't go on like this.'

104

'What did he do to make you call him an extortioner?'

'He asked me for money to ensure that my attendance here was made official. It's not of any great importance by itself.'

She looked at him as she sat in the bed. Her face, lit obliquely by the light from the bedside lamp, had an expression of quiet and domestic curiosity. 'I would have thought that very important,' she said. She was relaxed and comfortable; she had closed her eyes. 'How long have you been here?'

'I arrived here this morning.'

'Truthfully?' Her manner was suddenly incredulous, as though she could not believe this.

'Yes. Why shouldn't I be truthful about that?'

She still looked at him; perhaps he had said something which had been unwittingly odd. 'Well, you must be telling the truth, then, if you're as innocent as that, trying to make me believe what you say. Don't you know that there are all kinds of people here who try to claim that they have newly arrived, when in fact they have been here for far longer? Even when it's obvious to you – and they know it while they speak – that they have been here for months and even years? I don't think I exaggerate.' She paused. Her voice suggested that she was unused to speaking so much; the tiredness had come back into it. 'Why they pretend that they're newly arrived I don't know. Perhaps, by pretending to be new arrivals, they think that they may be able to appeal to an imagined soft-heartedness on the part of the servants. At the same time they forget that every minute of their lives within this house has been open to the scrutiny of the servants.' Despite her apparent tiredness there was a flow to her words which suggested that she had said something like this before. 'You aren't one of those, are you?' She did not wait for a reply. 'It doesn't work like that.' She pulled her nightgown about her shoulders and over her breast.

'No, I came here this morning. You can ask who you like about that.'

'I noticed that you said that Robert was only a servant. There was something about your tone of voice when you said: "only a servant".'

'Well, I meant it.'

'You must be new to say that.' She did not alter the tone of her voice. 'In a way, of course, he is only a servant. On the other hand the position of the servants is assured. Think of how that assurance helps them! They have an assurance, and because of that a certain security which gives them the opportunity to hold a kind of power; they can help visitors or not as they choose. At least, they could have the power to help you, if they would only trouble themselves to set about it. It's important to keep in with the servants; they can have a good deal of say in what happens. It doesn't do to belittle them.'

'Robert told me that.'

'In that case you ought to be grateful to him and to stop talking about him as though he were an extortioner. Don't you see that he was doing you a good turn in letting you know, beneath his breath as it were, how things stood? He was being very frank in his effort to help you when he said that it was important for you to keep up good relations with the servants here.'

'He didn't say it like that.' He lifted himself up on his elbows. 'If you interpret what he said like that, you might just as well argue that you are here, waiting for Robert, only because you hope that he might intercede as he could on your behalf.'

She paused to consider this. 'There's some truth in what you say.' She glanced at Alexander very directly, making the glance something more than it was. 'I'm not sure. If it were true, then it would be demeaning; perhaps it is. When I first met him he made his advances; partly because of his crudity I thought that I could get him to do what I wanted. I knew that he thought he was able to take advantage of me because I wanted him to help me. We both knew that. It was as good a way of beginning as any. I soon got used to this room. Even now he sometimes comes in and says: "I think I've found someone who can help you" and he knows full well that I no longer really believe him. He knows this and he laughs about it; it's a joke between us. In a way it's become a private thing.' She reached out to the stem of the lamp. 'I'll turn this out now.'

Alexander heard the click and the room was in darkness. 'Where's the importance in this?' He spoke from the wish to speak rather than to hear the reply.

'Never mind that. There's no meaning. When you've been here as long as I have you perhaps think that the servants have more power than they do. It might be one's own insecurity which makes for that impression.' She drew in her breath. 'All the same, one tries to get in with them. One tries to gain their approval.'

The silence was complete. When she spoke again her voice was unexpected. 'He keeps on promising that he'll arrange for me to get back to my home. He says he has influential friends in the town. He's not being untruthful. I said that it was a private joke between us. He's quite powerless because he doesn't know how to act, and because he's powerless he can promise anything. It needn't be reasonable; in fact it's easier to promise an unreasonable thing if one is powerless to promise anything; one doesn't have to invoke the fact of one's powerlessness. Anyway, it all comes to nothing.'

'I'll do what I can to help you.'

'Your voice is distinct in the darkness. What could you do? You aren't even a servant. You aren't even recognized by the servants.'

'No, I'm not a servant.'

'Then how can you help me? You can't even help yourself, or you wouldn't be here, lying on the floor.'

'Look,' said Alexander. 'Do you think I'm restrained in this house like a dog? I can do as I wish; when it's necessary for me to go back, then I'll go back. The same should apply to you: you aren't bound here. You are speaking nonsense, and from what you've said you are leading a life that will lead you nowhere.'

Her voice was quick. 'Be quiet for a minute.'

'What's the matter?' He said this rather loudly.

'Be quiet. He's coming up the stairs.'

A dreadful and artificial silence filled the room. For a moment Alexander felt like laughing: only at that moment had he realized what a ridiculous situation he had got himself into. He listened to the loud and uninflected voices outside on the landing, amused by their flat seriousness. The flimsy door was no impediment to sound, and he might have been able to distinguish the words had it not been for the diffuse echoes. The voices stopped and the door opened noisily. For the second time that night the glaring light was switched on.

Robert stood in the middle of the room. He did not look particularly drunk; he might not have been drinking at all. He looked at his watch and took it off. 'Three thirty,' he said. 'A bad day but a good evening. Even that could improve if you're in the mood.'

'Did you see the man at the railway?' Her voice was nonchalant.

'No. He never turned up. I did wait for him.' He said this with mock exasperation; the two of them might have been playing a game. 'I found someone, though, who might be useful. He says he might be able to get some tickets.'

'Who is he?'

'You wouldn't know him. I don't know him well myself, so I only hinted at what I wanted.' He spoke in a desultory manner. 'I've not kept you too long?'

'No. Of course not.'

Robert unbuttoned his shirt and took it off. His face was serious; he looked slightly angry. He looked round the room humourlessly, perhaps wondering where to throw the shirt. He saw Alexander's mattress. 'Who's that?' His voice was flat and transmitted the humourlessness and reinforced the impression of anger; at the same time it was difficult to tell whether or not this impression was intended.

'He's the one who came from the city this morning.'

108

'Oh. Him. Why have they put him in this room?'

'I don't know. I thought Mrs Killinger had mentioned it to you. He was here when I came in.'

'Why do they always choose my room for them? I might just go and see Apsleigh's assistant tomorrow.' He unhooked his belt. 'Is he asleep?'

'I don't know.'

'Not that that matters very much.' He pulled off his trousers and tossed them into the interior of a green steel locker, the door of which had been jammed open by a pile of books. He looked towards Alexander. 'You're asleep are you?' He grimaced at the mattress. 'It's all right. I don't expect you to speak.' He walked to the door and switched off the light. Before climbing into bed he half opened one of the windows.

Alexander, turning over and facing the wall, heard the private whispers. His dilemma was enhanced by his embarrassment; he could not stay in this room though he had been told that he must sleep here. Eventually he stood and folded his blankets and belongings in his arms. He was disregarded as he made his fumbling way to the door. Outside, on the landing, he found a strip of linoleum on which he might lie.

He was awake for much of the night, listening to the noise of the intermittent rain on the glass of the landing window. He was fitfully aware of people walking up and down the stairs and stepping over him. When he finally woke it was daylight. The landing, seen in daylight for the first time, was a draughty and dusty place, larger than it had seemed last night. He was cold. He searched for his coat. He was unable to find it. Anxious, now, he scrutinized the landing, an act which took a few seconds. He saw that the door of Robert's room was ajar; he must have left his coat in there, on the mattress. He pushed open the door. Inside, the room was larger than he remembered it. The room was empty; the bed was unmade and the door of the steel locker was still open. The air was close and vitiated although both the door and the window were open.

He was aware of his coldness. A wind blew up the angular stairwell, noisily, rustling the yellowed papers which hung, dog-eared, from drawing pins pushed into the baize of a notice board he had not seen last night. His jacket hung from the newel of the stair, but its pockets were empty.

He had lost his money, his letter, his diary, his keys, the railway ticket and his documents of identity.

As he ran down the stairs he saw Mr Turnbull's servant standing halfway up the flight. He rested one hand on the rail, this servant, and he looked upward. Alexander, afraid of him but wishing above all things to get past him (for he irrationally thought that if he retreated back to the landing he might demonstrate his fear to his own disadvantage), fled down the stairs, his hand in front of his face as though to protect himself from a blow.

The tall servant arrested his progress with the flat of his outstretched hand. Alexander staggered and would have fallen had not his arm been grasped.

'Let me alone!' cried Alexander.

'What are you afraid of? What are you flinching for?' There was a mixture of surprise and contempt in his voice.

'Flinch?' Alexander shook off his grip; the hand was withdrawn immediately. Alexander rubbed his wrist. He was aware that he had echoed a word without thinking. 'I've reason to hurry. Everything I have has been stolen.'

'Come down to the bottom of the stairs and tell me what you mean.'

'Grant me some intelligence, will you? I mean what I say.'

The servant raised his eyebrows as he diffidently observed Alexander. 'Did you sleep where you were told to?' he asked.

'No, that was impossible. I slept on the landing.'

The servant began to walk down the stairs. 'That's your concern, then. The corridors are very much common property. You have to accept what happens if you rest on the stairs or in the passages. You might have been safe had you stayed where you were directed. As it is, you can look for your possessions later. They might turn up. It's possible. Perhaps your belongings are mislaid. Possibly you've left them somewhere.' He gave out these platitudes rapidly and easily as though he wished to get them out of the way. 'At the moment I am instructed to advise you that my master wishes to see you.'

'Mr Turnbull?'

'His name is Mr Tompkins. I never met Turnbull; he was his predecessor.'

'Why does he want to see me?'

The servant, who had reached the bottom of the staircase, examined the prospect of the courtyard beyond the open door as though it was not very familiar to him. His stance showed that his patience was running out. 'I can do nothing more than to tell him that I've found you and that I have given you the message.'

Mr Tompkins sat in his chair. Nothing in his demeanour had changed; he still looked fatigued. He might have slept or he might not. He sat imperturbably with his ankles crossed. He expressed nothing; perhaps there was nothing unusual in his summoning a visitor at this early hour.

'Why did you call me?'

Mr Tompkins looked at him. 'What's happened? Your old supercilious complacence has gone.'

Alexander was angry at his detachment. 'What has happened? You're quick to recognize what you call a loss of complacence . . . I've been robbed of my belongings. I've lost everything I have.'

Mr Tompkins looked at him with a sudden acuity. 'Never mind what you've lost. That doesn't matter. Where's the letter? You've kept that safe?'

'The letter's lost, for what it's worth.'

Mr Tompkins stood up, quickly, everything in his

manner suggesting a quick and instinctive concern. 'You've lost that!'

His manner was infectious and quickened Alexander's heart beat. At that moment he thought he saw the letter's importance and the unredeemable nature of his loss. 'The letter's gone with the rest.' He glanced behind the standing man and saw the view of the town through the open window. 'Its subject was important; I know that now. But the letter itself; that hardly matters; I know exactly what it said . . .'

'*Where are your priorities!*'

Alexander had heard him shout before but this was unexpected; the fact fired a sudden fear; the transition from somnolence to this anxious shouting was too quick and beyond reasonable apprehension.

Alexander stood – he had left the door open, and he was aware that it was still open now; he was afraid lest the servants might be listening, and that Mr Tompkins' outburst might be overheard and misinterpreted. Mr Tompkins ran his fingers through his hair.

'Make sure you haven't got it with you.'

Alexander complied, though he knew in which pocket of his jacket the letter had lain. As he searched his clothes he knew that he did so only because he was being asked to.

'You've lost it then,' said Mr Tompkins.

'Have you ever had to write a reference?' asked Mr Tompkins.

'No,' said Alexander, cautiously. 'My position is too junior for that.' He might have added that the question had been a strange one.

'I asked that to make a point. Perhaps you could imagine yourself to be in the position of a man who has to write numerous references. Put yourself in his place as he considers what he will say about one man. He wishes to forward the career of his protégé but at the same time he knows he must retain his own integrity and honesty. He has to maintain his credibility as a referee for

112

the sake of other and future references he will write for candidates who are as yet unknown to him. Undue praise will lose him the confidence of those who examine the reference; an understated reference will damn his protégé and will undermine his own integrity. Again, no matter how accurately and truthfully he writes he is hesitant because he will never know for sure whether the holder of the reference will behave as he has behaved in the past: who knows what alteration may come over him?

'The spirit of a letter is somewhat similar, though my analogy is a poor one. When viewed in a certain light a letter has a certain semblance to a reference. The meaning is not so much in the literal content – that is fairly standard, and flows more or less along the lines set down by established precedent – but by the nuance, the studied synonym, the choice of set phrase. The sense lies not so much in the writing as in the style of writing and in the selection of emphasis. Each letter has, or seems to me to have, its different and unique intonation. One almost has the feeling that the writer of these letters does not know the person for whom they are intended (and by that I don't mean the initial recipient; he is in a sense no more than a bearer of a letter). One senses that the writer does not know the manner in which these letters will be finally interpreted; it is as if he only knew that the recipient's future must depend on the way in which the letters will be finally examined. That much is implicit in each one.

'I know your next question. You want to ask me if I know the names of those to whom you'll have to present the letter. I don't know the answer. Even if I did, and if I told you, you would be no better off; one couldn't suppose for a minute that they would be responsible for the final interpretation. I can't even begin to guess who these might be, and that fact makes me, as it has made the writer of the letter, cautious and circumspect. The uncertainty makes me anxious for you. When I read your letter I saw that the writer of it was anxious for you as well. I couldn't be certain whether his anxiety was specifically on your behalf, or whether it had to do with his own responsibility in writing a letter such as this.

'Against that background look at what has happened. Yesterday you tore that letter, acting in ignorance. Your action certainly altered the significance of the letter; despite the repairs to it, it was clear that it had been torn in anger – and what sort of impression do you expect that to give? Before that, don't you recall that I pointed out the creases where it had been refolded many times? That would have altered its sense, as would the thumb-prints and the other marks, the soiled edges and the smudged smuts from the railway when you opened it at the platform's edge.'

'But,' said Alexander, 'that letter was mine. I had no need to show it to anyone else.'

'On the contrary. You have a compulsive need to show it to other people. The letter itself by its staining and creasing showed that. Given the chance, who haven't you shown it to?'

'You're using my words to mean something I never intended.'

'I don't think that I am. Anyway, this is nothing but talk. You'll never get your letter back. What are you going to do about it?'

'There's not much I can do,' said Alexander.

'For your own peace of mind,' said Mr Tompkins, 'I should write out the letter word for word as you remember it. Close your eyes in thought, as you write, and recall the script exactly as it was. You have looked at it often enough. You ought to be able to remember the typewriter face, the spacing, the indentation of the paragraphs . . . all the time you should be as truthful as you can be: alter nothing and add nothing.

'You ought to do this as soon as possible, before you start to change the sense of it in your own mind.

'Try to copy the signature, and write the word "facsimile" beneath it to make it obvious that you are not committing a fraud but merely making an *aide-*

114

mémoire; your letter will be seen as a copy and you must state the fact yourself, or else you'll find that deception will be imputed to you.

'You might consider writing an addendum of your own, stating what happened to the original; if you do this you must be truthful; you must say that you lost the original as you did, sleeping albeit in ignorance in a place to which vagrants and undesirables had easy access.'

'People roam about the house at night, then?'

'They say so.' A new thought had crossed Mr Tompkins' mind. 'Do you recall the typewriter face?'

'Is that why you called me this morning?'

'No. I didn't know then that you had lost the letter.'

'Then why did you summon me?'

Mr Tompkins sat back in his chair as though resigned to his weariness. 'It hardly matters now, in the face of events.'

'Surely it does; it does to me. You've gone out of your way to help me. I was thinking of that last night. At first I thought Mrs Killinger was able to give me help, but . . .'

'Why do you keep on mentioning these names to me?' Mr Tompkins closed his eyes. 'How often do I have to tell you that I don't know their names?'

'Why did you summon me? You must have had something important to say to have summoned me at such an early hour.'

Mr Tompkins leaned forward. 'It was important. It seemed very important then. Less so now. I called for you this morning because I felt that I had some clue as to the significance of the letter. However, I needed to see the letter itself to verify my suspicions.'

'What suspicions?' Alexander found the other man's tone serious, and he wondered why this was so. This must have been apparent in his face.

'You're not regarding this as a game then?'

'I assure you that I don't regard it as a game.'

'Will you listen to what advice I can give, inconclusive as it is?'

'Yes. I can't see what else I can do.'

'Listen to me now, then. Go down to the town and find a scribe. I call them by that name because that is what they are. I told you about them before, I remember. You'll need a good one; there are many of them and they all differ in their ability. Perhaps you should select advice as to which of them you should choose: but, at all events, find a good one. It's difficult for me to give any advice about this choice, but I've been told that one may gain an impression from the range of advertisements which each holds in the window of his premises. I'm uncertain of the truth of this, but I am told that most of the advertisements depict type-writer faces and samples of letters. One thing I know is that one must avoid the premises of a man who displays a large number of faces in his window. As I have said (and I know this for certain) the displayed placards of types are in the windows only to advertise; the best scribes are those who rely on personal recommendation and who need no advertisement. Their shops will probably be not marked in any way. The best of them follow their calling out of interest and not for profit; these men of course never advertise because they make their living in other ways.

'The choice may be difficult to make.' Mr Tompkins held up his hands as if to indicate that he was only speaking from hearsay and without any direct experience of what he was saying. 'On the one hand a scribe who possesses a wide variety of types may bewilder you with choice. On the other, a man who has a limited range may have nothing which fits your recall.' He leaned back and looked at Alexander and grasped his arm as though he might be about to say something of importance. 'I must warn you. Don't spend too long looking at the typefaces or you'll find that the selection of print will blur the memory of your own letter. In such circumstances confabulation comes easy.'

A question framed itself in Alexander's mind; as he asked this question he felt that he was losing the point of what Mr Tompkins had been saying. He felt himself to be ingenuous and naïf. 'I had no idea that it might be so complicated.'

'What do you mean? The copying of the letter is less

complicated than the understanding of the original.'

'Why should the typewriter face matter so much?'

Mr Tompkins, instead of becoming irritated by the question, as Alexander had half expected, nodded his head as though a salient point had been raised. 'I see that you are beginning to understand,' he said. 'That's good; you've an eye for these things. In fact I believe the typeface to be of little importance. Perhaps it has received the emphasis it has because it is obvious. It is, after all, no more than the outer appearance of the vehicle used for expressing the words. At the same time it's as well to be on the safe side. I say that for two reasons. Firstly, though the face may seem to be obviously apparent but of little importance, yet it may have an unsuspected significance. Secondly, should your letter be borderline (if it is such a letter) – do you follow me? – then the typeface may well be critical. Only one thing is certain; the copy should be as near a facsimile of the original as is possible.

'One must weigh up all possibilities. After your copy has been made you will have to submit it to the receiving authorities. Supposing after that the original turns up in their hands. The two will certainly be compared. Looked at like that the honesty of the copy is of utmost importance.'

Mr Tompkins stood and walked towards the window. 'For all that I have been saying, I urge you to do one thing. Be honest in all that you do. Make your copy as you would have it received; don't pass off your copy as the real thing. Perhaps I'm telling you something which is obvious, but don't lie or prevaricate to the scribe, or he'll surely put some condemnatory mark in your duplicate letter which you won't even realize is there. For the same reason I advise you to pay him well, to stint nothing, and to veil your impatience if you should think that he is being dilatory and wasting time which you have paid for.'

'I have no money! That was stolen too.'

'What work do you do?'

'I know no-one here; how could I find work?'

'Here.' Mr Tompkins took a card from his pocket. 'It's a kind of stop-gap. Take it.'

Alexander took the card; it looked like an ordinary visiting card. There was nothing remarkable about it except the name. The lines of print were unornamented. 'What will this do for me?'

'Show it to one of the servants, as you call them that. The card means nothing except that I'll act as your guarantor.'

'But the name on the card is "Turnbull".'

'Well, what of that? He was my predecessor, the man who hoarded things as though he were here for an eternity. I'm aware of my own position; I never bothered to have my own visiting cards printed.'

'Well,' Alexander looked at the card and put it in the back pocket of his trousers.

The room was silent; Mr Tompkins seemed to feel no particular wish to conclude the interview. He sat down and looked out of the window.

Alexander waited for him to speak, but when he did not he walked closer to the window. 'May I ask you a direct question?'

'Yes, you may.'

'Is it possible for me to return to my city?'

'Of course it is. This is a civilized country, so they say. What could prevent your return if you wished to go back? The distance is nothing if the desire to travel is strong enough.'

Alexander was about to speak, but the other man held up his hand. 'Wait for me to finish,' he said, but then he fell silent. He stood up again and began to pace the room, his face thoughtful. He held his hands together behind his back. Alexander noticed for the first time that his wrists and hands were very thin and that his fingers were very long. For some unidentifiable reason he found himself looking fixedly at Mr Tompkins' hands, as though he saw them as being less like the hands of a living man than the elongated hands of a gothic

118

sculpture in their pallor and narrow length. This was a transient impression; Mr Tompkins' hands might have been anatomically unusual but there was nothing abnormal about them.

'Do you think you will return?' asked Mr Tompkins. 'Do you think that you could resume your past life?'

Although this last question was unexpected, Alexander grasped the significance of it immediately. He knew that at the moment he was most unwilling to return to his past work, and that his unwillingness increased with every hour. He had only spent two days away from his old place of work, but even in that short space of time he had been able to take a detached view of it, as though merely because of distance he had been given the facility of regarding his past life as though he were observing the past life of someone else. He saw with a barbed detachment (which may or may not have been inaccurate) the routine mode of a routine life with ambitions which were no longer worth while. He saw his teachers as being less than the complete men he had supposed them to be. He wondered what would happen in the future.

'What are you thinking?' asked Mr Tompkins. His voice was compassionate and unintrusive as though he had already divined Alexander's thoughts.

'It scarcely matters.'

The other man slowly nodded his head. He walked to the window.

'When I first came here,' said Alexander, 'I was told to look for an official course of instruction. I realize that that doesn't matter now.' (He laid emphasis on the word 'official'.) 'The only thing which remains true is that I am looking for instruction and advice. You said that that letter was important. I didn't believe you at first. It was the letter which took me away from the city and in so doing allowed me to see myself as though I were another person. I don't think I could go back to my past life.'

'What do you propose to do? Have you any provision for the future?'

'I need your advice. I'm in a foreign place, and from what I see of it it is not rational. The servants don't act like rational people. One begins to feel very vulnerable after a time. I don't know what will happen in the future.' He paused, and looked down at his own hands, marvelling at the contrast between them and the attenuated hands of the other man. 'Will you listen to me if I tell you of my life in the city?'

'I'll gladly listen, but you must be faint with hunger; you haven't eaten since yesterday.'

'That doesn't matter. I was hungry earlier; not now.'

'Well, tell me things you want to tell me. Keep private the things you wish to keep to yourself. I ask you to do that because I am only a man like yourself; I have no special qualifications and I'm neither a confessor nor a doctor. I can only help you out of what one might call a spirit of humanity, though the phrase has a ring of pomposity about it. My advice may be faulty and incomplete.'

'I worked in a government laboratory in the city. A last-century building in the university precinct, near the canal; an impressive building in a heavy way.'

'I've never been to the city. I don't know it, but I don't suppose the exterior of the building matters very much.'

'No, of course not. I was trying to arrange things in my own mind. At one time the work could have been important. Even now I regard it as being of interest if not importance. In a way we could have been working on any subject. The important facts as I see them now, in retrospect . . .' He saw that Mr Tompkins was looking out of the window. His gaze had a fixed expression, exactly as it had done on the occasion of Alexander's first visit. Alexander felt irritated that he had lost Mr Tompkins' attention.

'I'm afraid that I'm not expressing myself very well,' said Alexander. Without waiting for any reply or comment he continued. 'No, what mattered then, and what I failed to see while I worked there, was that the department itself was of more importance than either the work

120

which was done or the people who worked. Perhaps that doesn't make much sense, but it's an impression I found. Had no-one worked there, had no work been carried out and nothing original done, the department would still exist in name, organized by its administrative staff. It was a self-interested and introverted place. The things that mattered were its status and reputation. Its senior members spent most of their time travelling, often abroad, trying to sell the name of the department. The amount of original work was negligible. The standing of the place was all-important.'

'You speak in the past tense.'

'That's true.' His voice was surprised. 'I hadn't realized that until now.' At the same time he felt pleased that Mr Tompkins had been listening to him, despite his appearance of giving his whole concentration to what was happening in the valley beyond the window. 'I don't intend to go back there.'

'I see.'

'I've made up my mind about that.' He followed Mr Tompkins' gaze; the two men stood side by side, both of them staring out of the window, though nothing was happening in the town below them.

'Don't you think you're being hard on yourself?' Mr Tompkins, while he spoke, followed the moving plume of steam from a distant railway train. The train approached them over the plain at the mouth of the valley; it was still a long way off. It must have been visible in the distance for some time. 'Perhaps you ought to consider things before you make emphatic statements.'

'You may be right. It's difficult to say. I only know that, were I to go back, I would be a different person. My ambitions would have changed; I feel sure of that.'

'I suppose that's inevitable.'

'There are a number of questions I want to ask you.'

Mr Tompkins turned to look at him; his action was coincidental with the disappearance of the moving track of steam, so that it was difficult for Alexander to determine whether Mr Tompkins looked at him out of interest or out of default. 'Yes,' he said. 'But there is all the time in the world for that. Your first priority should be to reconstruct your letter before the recall of its sense is lost to you.'

'You're still talking about the letter. I had begun to think that our talk had become more rational.'

'It's common to think that different standards and foreign procedures are irrational. You've seen this town and you've listened to me; you ought to have recognized by now that the people who live here work and think in accordance with standards very different from your own. I'm not suggesting that you should accept those standards. It's enough that you recognize them. The things you consider significant may have no significance here, and, conversely, the things which happen here should not be dismissed merely in the light of your own experience. Such things may be of extreme importance.'

Alexander felt again the familiar sense of an impasse. Yesterday he would have felt exasperation and an irritation at the way in which statements were thrust at him, as though he were a child. Now he was aware of the beginnings of patience. 'I have to trust you,' he said. 'I have to trust you; I have a kind of faith in you, though why that should be . . .' He took the card from his pocket and looked at the name which was remarkable only because it was obsolete. He wondered what Mr Turnbull had been like, and whether he was still alive. He wondered why Mr Turnbull had had these cards printed, and whether he would have resented the second-hand use of his name. 'I'll do as you suggest.'

It was while he was walking down the familiar street which led to the town that he discovered the reasons for his sudden regard for Mr Tompkins. His discovery made him quicken his pace, for he was anxious to act on his mentor's advice as soon as possible. He recalled the letter in his mind's eye; he thought he could remember it accurately, word for word. His discovery was this: at no time had Mr Tompkins attempted to impress him with his superior knowledge of the town or the system by which it worked. He had never treated Alexander as a client; he had never appealed to conscience. He had never acted other than as a friend or ally. He had taken Alexander's outbursts of anger and exasperation with a reasoned and tolerant understanding.

Alexander, feeling more at ease than he had felt since he had first seen the envelope lying on the tablecloth, began to search for a man to whom he could dictate the letter. He put it to himself that it did not matter that he did not understand the importance of what he was doing in this action. It was a novel experience, doing something which was, on the face of it, unreasonable, merely because he had been advised to do it. Perhaps it gave him a sense of diminished responsibility. Whether this was true or not he had a faith in the future, whatever it might hold.

In his pocket he had a wad of banknotes, money borrowed from Mrs Killinger. He had met her in the servants' kitchen. The loan of the money had contravened no authority. The promissory note had been signed and witnessed and the visiting card had been pinned to it with a long dressmaker's pin. The money had been counted out twice, in old notes, crumpled and worn and which seemed to occupy a far greater volume than their monetary worth warranted. The door to the safe had been locked. Mrs Killinger had even told him of a man who might be expected to give sound advice about finding a reliable copyist.

The one thing that dwelt at the back of his mind was the knowledge that he was in debt. He owed the servants a good deal of money; far more, in fact, than he had expected, not only in the repayment of the loan (on which interest had to be paid) but also in respect of gratuities incurred for all kinds of small services which, at the time, had seemed like small acts of kindness.

Mrs. Killinger's friend was an unprepossessing man who appeared to be without work and without any ambition or intention of gaining any. Alexander found him sitting on a bench in an alley which ran under the north side of the church. He was dressed in faded black. His suit was tailored as though for an old man even though the wearer could not have been older than forty. He was drunk. A half-empty cider bottle stood on the bench by his side. The bench itself seemed to be a haunt of local alcoholics, for behind it was a litter of bottles and rags. The man caught Alexander's glance.

'Do you know Mrs Killinger?' asked Alexander.

The man nodded his head quietly. Suspicion had been evident in his every movement until Alexander had spoken. 'What do you want?'

Alexander, looking at him, was aware that he himself must look dirty and unshaven. 'She said that I ought to see you about something.'

'She did, did she? I hardly know her. She's one of the charity women from the church.'

Alexander looked down at him. His contempt must have shown itself, for the man began to shake his head drunkenly. 'You're all the same,' he said. He pulled his coat about him. Alexander noticed that the side of his face was dusty and grazed as though he had recently fallen. 'I don't suppose you'd have the price of a cup of tea about you?' He put a hand to his damaged cheek and looked at his fingers fixedly, as though he was surprised not to see blood.

'Mrs Killinger told me that you might know of a man who would copy a letter.' Alexander was unwilling to use the word 'scribe' as Mr Tompkins had done; the word seemed so ludicrously antique.

'So you want a scribe, do you? You might as well speak plainly. I understand what you mean; I wasn't always sitting on this bench.' His face held an expression of resignation and, inexplicably, a coy diffidence. 'Did she say that I might know of one?'

'She did. If you are Mr Tarrant.'

'You say that in a very off-hand way. Mr Tarrant!' He spoke his name with a downward inflection of sneering deprecation. 'There was a Mr Tarrant here once. He gave out charity as well, and sat on this bench, talking to

124

those who would listen. Where is he now?' He looked down at the ground and pressed the tips of a forefinger and thumb against his closed eyes. He suddenly looked up. His eyes were unexpectedly clear. 'Are you a student?'

'No.'

'Oh, then. That's more like it. So you want a scribe?'

Alexander had taken some money out of his pocket. He sensed that the man was aware of this even though he had not looked at the action.

'Well, you might do worse than visit Sleight, if that's the case. He's done me a good turn or two in the past.'

Alexander had it in mind to remark that the good turns of this man Sleight did not appear to have been beneficial. He said something to this effect. His words put the sitting man into a silent rage. 'You're the fool, then, if you think that.'

'So you'd recommend this man you call Sleight?'

'For what it's worth, yes.' He shook his head. 'I only know that he's a scribe because I've been in his shop. Who isn't out for himself? Sleight's a pawnbroker. Who do I know who'd trust him? Hey?' He laid vehemence into his words. He looked up into Alexander's face, and then downwards to the hand which held the coins. 'You're too cocky. I can see you holding that money, and in the way you do, waiting until you've got your information. I suppose you think you pity me. You! Yes, I've heard of you. I lived up in that house for long enough; I know what you are. I know that you're blind enough to pity me, just because I asked you for the price of a cup of tea. I can imagine what state you're in, even if you can't see it yourself.'

'Tea. That's a fine euphemism.'

'Well, then. So that's the tune is it? Keep your money. Besides, I wouldn't want what you offer me now, when you are in the state you are. Who knows where your money's come from and who it belonged to? As for you, you must be up to your eyes in debt.

'Yes,' he continued, seeing the shame in Alexander's

face. 'You are young enough for that to get you. You're young enough to pity me. I'm a free man. I owe nothing to a soul: there's no-one that wants anything from me.'

'How do you pay for your drink?'

'Keep your students' questions to yourself.'

Alexander held out the silver coin.

'I take it you won't want this back?' He looked slyly up at the young man. He made as if to throw the coin with all his strength over the high wall of the alley. He looked at the coin as it lay in the palm of his hand. 'Who did this originally belong to?' He seemed to be asking the question of himself; then he looked instinctively down the sloping alley to the cobbled street which led to the dark quarter of the town. 'I don't owe anything to a soul,' he repeated, and two streaks of maudlin wetness fell down his cheeks.

Sleight's shop, the pawnbroker's, hung its three balls out into the narrow street like planets in an urban sky. Alexander had no wish to go inside. He had walked past the shop twice, reluctant to enter. The street was half-familiar; it was a city street, out of place in this town. Coal smoke rolled out of the high cowls and the daylight was half obscured.

In the street he met a man he recognized by sight. It was only after he looked again that he saw him as being Mr Mause, the man who had once given him a book which had long since been lost. He walked up to him and touched him on the arm.

Mr Mause did not recognize Alexander; he saw his unshaven and unwashed state and pulled his arm away.

'Wait, sir,' Alexander held out his hands.

Mr Mause looked at him, still without recognition, automatically putting his hand in his pocket as though to give money to a beggar.

'No, I only want to ask you something.'

'What is it?' asked the doctor, surprised. 'I think I know you. You've changed.'

'I have been told to find a person to copy a letter.'

126

'Oh! You're one of those! You want a scribe, you mean.' The doctor's manner relaxed. 'I'm hardly the man to give you advice. It's never been necessary for me to see one.' He cast a glance at the pawnbroker's shop as though indicating that he had never needed the services of that particular shop either. 'They say there's not much to choose between them.' He would have continued walking if Alexander had not called him back.

'But have you heard anything; anything perhaps in conversation?'

Mr Mause pointed to the pawnbroker's sign. 'He's reckoned to be a fair man. He's a member of the Jacksonian Club, and that may mean something in this town. I don't know the man personally, but . . .' He shrugged his shoulders. 'I take it you want a letter drafted from memory?'

'That's exactly it.'

'He may be able to help you then.'

Mr Mause stopped talking abruptly and walked away, up the street, staring down at the pavement as though Alexander had given him something to think about.

Alexander watched him as he walked. It was impossible for him not to wonder where he was going. His figure was solitary and precise and there was a briskness to his pace. Alexander watched him turn a far corner, and then, suddenly, he opened the door of the pawnshop and entered.

Mr Sleight stood behind the counter. The opening of the shop door caught his attention. He stood, unmoving, as though he had been in the act of carrying out some unspecified but intricate clerical task, but had been rendered motionless by the opening of the door. He was short and his face was smooth-shaven. His cheeks and his neck were fat. The tortoiseshell arms of his spectacles had drawn grooves along the fatty flesh of his temples. He was dressed in a black jacket of an obsolete government pattern. He said nothing but watched Alexander.

127

Alexander silently looked up at the racks of hanging suits, the shelves of mantel clocks and drawing-room ornaments, the trays of rings and watches which had never been redeemed and which were inclined behind the window. He looked at the ledger on the dusty counter. Apart from the ledger and a brass inkstand and a tin of moth repellant (he found himself reading the name on the label) the counter was empty.

'Do you wish to pawn something?' Mr Sleight's voice was severe. He gave the appearance of having resumed his clerical task at the ledger, though his eyes peered over it, observant and critical.

'No, I don't.'

'Why are you here, then?'

Alexander felt such a profound distaste for both the man and the room that he was on the verge of walking out of the shop. Obscurely he noticed that there had not been the least trace of an echo to the pawnbroker's words, as though the thick lines of hanging garments had the property of absorbing all sound at the moment of utterance. The atmosphere was musty, like the interior of a long-locked wardrobe.

'What do you want?' Mr Sleight no longer made a pretence of looking at his ledger.

Alexander was about to speak, but he hesitated and did not get the opportunity to do so. A woman entered the shop, and, without a moment's hesitation, she held up a suit and laid it on the counter for valuation. The fact that it was a modern suit, badly cut and tailored, seemed incongruous; everything else in the shop had the appearance of being old.

The transaction was so swift that Alexander scarcely saw the ticket and the money change hands. Then the woman had gone, and the only evidence for the visit was the suit itself, now draped over Mr Sleight's arm.

'You're still here?' Mr Sleight was pinning a label to the lapel of the coat. Then something dawned in his mind. He smiled slightly. He passed his hand over the material of the suit as though stroking fur and not wool.

His expression had changed; his severity had gone. 'Ah. I think I see what you want.'

'Yes. I wish to have a letter copied.'

'I wondered if that might be the case.' Mr Sleight hung up the suit on a rack with a dozen others and then leaned over the counter, holding out his hand. He shook hands with Alexander who, seeing him more closely, noticed that the broker's obsolete government suit was shiny at the shoulders and that the lapels and cuffs were orna-mented by black braiding.

'You must tell me about your letter,' he said. 'I'm glad you came here.' He pulled his hand from Alexander's grasp and wiped it on the front of his own jacket, feeling the black braiding with his fingers. He lifted up the flap of the counter. 'Is it a long letter?'

'No, not long. But it may be complicated.'

The broker lowered his head and pursed his lips, weighing up the simple statement as though it might contain some hidden convolution. 'Yes,' he said at length, 'they are all complex. You're telling the truth there.' He opened the door at the rear of the shop and, almost deferentially, ushered Alexander through it. He held out his hand, palm uppermost, to indicate a chair which stood in front of a table from which the breakfast plates were not yet cleared.

Alexander sat down and watched the movements of the broker as he closed the door to the shop and walked to the newel post of a narrow stairway that ascended in a match-boarded recess in the darkness of a corner of the room.

'Ann,' the broker called. 'Ann. Come down here, will you?'

There was the sound of footsteps on the floor above. Someone familiar with the darkness descended the stairs.

'Will you mind the shop?' The broker's words were quiet; Alexander had difficulty making them out through the muffling rows of hanging clothes. 'I have someone with me in the back room.'

While he had been listening to Mr Sleight, Alexander had looked round the back room, and had observed the close-packed racks and the cluttered shelves. A square iron stove with mica windows stood against the chimney-breast and opposite the stove a window allowed a little light into the cluttered room.

A young woman, visibly pregnant, stood at the bottom of the stairwell. She crossed the room and opened the door to the shop. She cast a dismissive glance at both Alexander and the broker as though she wished nothing to do with either of them.

'Ann, close that door, will you?' Mr Sleight's voice was solicitously low.

The door was closed with abrupt impatience.

Mr Sleight shook his head and pursed his lips again, perhaps ashamed that a small domestic scene should have happened in the presence of a third person.

'Was that your daughter?' Alexander spoke out of the need to break the silence.

'Daughter-in-law.' Mr Sleight looked at the table before he sat down opposite Alexander. He carefully lifted the plates and the cups and stacked them to the side of the table; he did this with a studied manner as though he were putting an indiction on his household. Once he had sat down his manner altered. He looked at his watch. 'Now, I ought to say at the outset that my time is a valuable commodity. After all,' he said, as if he were about to make a joke, 'I've had one heart attack already, and I've high blood pressure and refuse to take the medicine prescribed for it because it makes me feel ill. The doctor is worried about high blood sugar. So I haven't long. In truth my time is valuable. The shorter the time left, the more valuable it becomes. Do you agree?' He said this as though it were a pleasantry he had said many times before.

Alexander listened without sympathy. 'Yes, I suppose you could argue that,' he said, lightly, aware that the broker required no particular comment.

'Let's begin. The first item will be to decide the hourly

rate for this commission.' Mr Sleight held a pocket book in his left hand. 'It saves trouble to decide this in advance.'

Alexander nodded. Despite himself and despite his first impressions he found the broker's presence not as unwelcome as he had expected. He was aware that Mr Sleight was staring at him. 'What's your usual rate?'

The broker stated his rate; his eyes were candid and frank. The terms were a statement. Alexander was in no position to disagree with them.

'Very well, then.'

The broker began to explain his work in a very practical way. He set out a scheme for the task which lay ahead, emphasizing the need for order and continuity. He asked tangential questions, as a thorough physician will ask questions which bear no relation to the complaint.

'You may have told me before, but who did you say advised you to seek the services of a scribe?'

'Tompkins.'

'Mr Tompkins.' He placed an emphasis on the man's title, implying that Alexander ought to have used that title too. 'I've heard people speak of him.' He licked the point of his pencil.

'Mr Tompkins says that the typeface is all-important.' Alexander, though unwilling to give Mr Sleight any offence, felt obliged to carry out Mr Tompkins' instructions.

The broker leaned his head to one side, in the manner of a man considering the validity of a minor point. 'He's right, of course. That's by the way; you can only listen to one adviser, and it might as well be myself now that you have commissioned my time.' Unconsciously he put the point of the pencil to his lips again, dampening the lead with his tongue. 'We must begin by being prosaic. We'll draft a copy in entirety, exactly as the recall comes to you, not bothering about errors or omissions. Doubtless there will be many corrections and alterations, but we need not consider them while we are constructing that first draft. It is the most important one, that first draft, although we shall destroy it when the final draft is completed.' He looked directly at Alexander. 'I take it that you will stint nothing in order to obtain a final letter which is as exact a facsimile as it is possible to make?'

There had been something about Mr Sleight's manner which had inspired Alexander's confidence. The broker was not making light of the letter. 'Yes,' said Alexander, 'that is right. That is what I want above all things.'

'Good.' Mr Sleight sat back in his chair. 'Then, between you and me, I can tell you that you have been guided to the right man. Between us we will finish this task in a professional manner. I saw that you were a perceptive man when you wisely said that your letter might be complex.' He sat squarely and capably at the table. He reached out his hand and touched the cold teapot, but his words had been confident. He was an expert practitioner who expected respect.

The complexity of recalling the exact format of the letter was a much more difficult task than Alexander could ever have imagined. Sleight had been very patient and he had guided Alexander through phrase after phrase until the first draft had been completed. The small and stuffy back room had become almost unbearably hot; beads of sweat stood out on the broker's brow and he constantly put his fingers to his shirt collar as though he found it uncomfortable. Long ago he had rolled up his sleeves. He had said that the first draft would be unsatisfactory and so it was. It contained more of the broker's prompting than Alexander's recall. When Alexander pointed this out he was told that it did not matter. This draft, after all, was only a framework, as it were, upon which the meaning of the letter should be hung. It was nothing more than a review of the codified systems of the original letter.

Of the two, the broker had the greater patience. He would willingly retrack, making marginal notes and little reference marks as he went back to fine details which Alexander thought had long ago been solved. His slow methodical manner was suited to his patient task.

They took half an hour for lunch, a hasty meal of sandwiches prepared by Sleight's daughter-in-law. The girl sent out for a jug of beer paid for by Alexander. They sat on their uncomfortable bent-wood chairs, eating without speaking. While he ate the broker reviewed his notes, doggedly determined to continue his task.

He demonstrated his practised shrewdness in a personal way, as though he were a family lawyer of long acquaintance. Alexander was at first suspicious of his approach, sensing it to be merely a professional quality that he might affect when speaking to any client. As time drew on he grew to accept Sleight's bland confidentiality.

Alexander was forced to smile when he considered that, only a few hours ago, he had thought that the preparation of a facsimile of the letter would have been a simple and straightforward thing. He could well see now that nothing could have been further from the truth.

Once he wondered whether the broker's continued insistence on the exactitude of Alexander's recall over one ill-remembered phrase might not be a device for wasting time and gaining a larger commission; a moment later he felt guilty that he had ever thought this. Sleight's depth of concentration surely precluded the thought of his own gain. In retrospect when he looked back at that phrase he saw that it was indeed of importance because it qualified and made ambiguous the sentence in which it occurred. He suggested that they go back to it and Mr Sleight very patiently did so, remarking that it was indeed an odd phrase and unsatisfactory either in or out of context and suggesting that it might never have been in the original at all. He worked with a methodical skill.

He pressed Alexander to stay to dinner. It was imperative that the letter should be drafted at a single sitting, he said, otherwise so much material would be forgotten and lost beyond retrieval; if the delay was as short as a single night, so much ground would be lost and so much invented matter remembered in place of the original, that the task would be all the harder. Accordingly, even though the stuffiness of the room was beginning to make him feel sick, Alexander stayed for dinner, a rather indifferent meal with too much potato and cabbage and cooked by Sleight's daughter-in-law. While they ate their dinner, Sleight's daughter-in-law (who said that she was not hungry) walked about the room in a bemused fashion, scarcely noticing either Alexander or her father-in-law; she seemed to be preoccupied with her pregnancy, though even that might have been doubtful: once, Alexander, attempting to make conversation with her, asked her when the baby was due. In response to this the girl shrugged her shoulders and said she did not know, that she did not know the dates and that they had said nothing to her at the clinic.

In the early evening her husband came home. He sat for some time at the end of the table, watching the construction of the letter and looking alternately at his father and at Alexander, saying nothing but intruding his presence in the fashion of a man watching a game of chess played by two bad players. Eventually he tired of the monotony of this. He stood and walked to a black-framed mirror which hung on the chimney-breast above the stove. He began to brush his hair.

The girl looked up from her abdomen and stared at him. 'You're going out, are you?'

'Yes.' He continued to look at his reflection. 'I don't suppose I shall be long. It depends if I meet anyone I know.'

'I've got rights as well!' said the girl, rather sharply.

Mr Sleight overheard this; he fell silent in mid-sentence. He turned away from the table and looked at his daughter-in-law. He loosened his collar. He seemed to have forgotten his client for the moment. 'What rights have you got?' His tone of voice was weary (as though the girl had said something tediously stupid) but his face was red and ill-tempered.

'I've got my rights.'

134

'I've got my rights!' he said, mimicking her flat voice. Then he began to shout, unexpectedly. 'No one has a right! There is no such thing as a right!' He brought the palm of his hand down on the mass of paper which lay over the surface of the table. 'They're always talking about rights as though they existed. Not one of us has the right to draw his next breath.'

During this tirade he had become angry but it was easy to see that his words had had no effect at all on the girl. Directly he turned back to the papers she looked away from him and examined her finger-nails with a lustreless gaze. The young man still stared at his own pale face in the mirror. 'I shall be off, then. I shan't be long. We'll see what happens.'

The broker turned again and began shouting. 'Can't you see that you've both been actively disturbing us? Can't you see that this is important work? Can't you leave us in peace?'

They were alone again and again work began in earnest. They were both fatigued and even the broker admitted that he was beginning to see the papers as though through a haze. The room was hot. Early drafts and working sheets had been periodically shovelled into the fire for, as Mr Sleight said, it was important that nothing should remain except the final fair copy of the letter.

It was nearly three in the morning by the time the broker had finished and had led the way through the shop and had unbolted and unlocked the shop door. He and Alexander stood at the threshold of the door, looking out into the night. They both seemed to be pleased by what they had accomplished. Mr Sleight held the simple brown envelope in his hand. He held it between the finger and thumb of his right hand and it caught the light of the lamps in the shop. In that light the envelope, by its appearance, its size, and the format of the name and address upon it seemed to be more than a reproduction of the original. 'I think you'll find that I've given you good service. I hope you feel that you have had value for your money.' The broker's voice was prosaic and unexpected in the silence.

Alexander was faint with exhaustion. 'I'm grateful to you,' he said.

'You shouldn't be. You have done the work. You found me, and the letter came from your memory.' He craned his head out into the street. 'You've been a good man to work for. I think you knew what you wanted.' He looked at Alexander. 'I would say that, in general, things do not go as easily. It's been a pleasure to work with you.' His breath smoked in the cold. He was still dressed in shirt-sleeves and he shivered slightly. He seemed to be anxious to get back inside. 'I only wish that the majority of people who came to see me were like yourself.'

When Alexander arrived back at the house, towards four o'clock in the morning, he had become so absorbed with the abstract idea of rest that he had paid no attention as to where he might sleep. An hour ago he had given his full concentration to the reconstruction of the letter and, when that had been completed, to the examination of the copy to check its accuracy against the confused memory in his own mind. There had been no room for any other thought then; now, alone, he was able to piece together the events of the day and he saw that there was little to sustain him. He was dissatisfied with his reduplication of the letter. During his walk from the broker's shop small omissions and inconsistencies had kept recurring in his mind; he was not sure whether they were factual, or due to Mr Sleight's suggestion, or even whether they had their root in the fact that he had been thinking about the subject for too long: this troubled him, for he was beginning to find that, after the mental effort of the day, he could no longer remember the original letter clearly. Perhaps, under the broker's guidance, he had concentrated so hard on details, that he had neglected and omitted important passages of the letter, in the same way that an inexpert signwriter, in his earnest attempt to space the characters equally and to

136

convey the appearance of their equal height, may neglect and omit passages of the work he has been set to copy. Alexander had worked all day in Mr Sleight's house with a slavish eye at the recall of small facts. Now, alone, he saw as if from afar his mistakes. The reduplicated letter might just as well have been an invention, a copy only in point of style. The original was lost to him. He would have liked to believe that this loss was temporary, due to tiredness, but he was not sure whether this was true.

He opened the door from the courtyard to the stair-case of the wooden buildings. A fluctuating moonlight suffused the hallway and the stairs beyond. To the left, in a recess which must previously have escaped his attention, an oak-cased time-recording clock kept time with a solemn tick. The sound pervaded the quiet air. There was just enough light to see its face; the two hands were approaching the hour of four, and, as the minute hand reached the hour, the mechanism emitted a series of soft shuffling clicks before the slow beat reasserted itself.

He walked up the stairs to the landing. A steel-framed bed had been erected on the linoleum floor, its head against the hand-rail that ran from the newel post to the wall. The bed was unexpected, standing as it did on the little landing; it was difficult to conceive a less likely place for a bed. It almost filled the floor space and there was hardly room to get round it. Had Alexander been running up the stairs he would have collided with it.

The bed was made and its covers were turned down. Alexander saw, for the first time, that it rested in the place where he had slept last night; its head was ori-ented in the same direction as his body had been. The moon was bright enough to see that some objects were laid out on the counterpane in a row, as though awaiting identification or recognition by their owner. They com-prised Alexander's keys, a railway ticket, a diary, a comb and a folding pocket razor such as was used by travellers. The last two things did not belong to

Alexander and there was no means of telling where they came from. He searched on the counterpane for his original letter, though he knew in his heart that it would not be there. Half unconsciously – his mind had reverted to an aspect of one phrase which he had been discussing with Mr Sleight – he began to undress. He took off his shoes and placed them, by feel, in the shadows against the wall under the notice board where the pinned papers were obscurely visible. He was still half dressed when he got into bed. He was still wakeful; he sat forwards, peering into the darkness; the moon was obscured and a wind had arisen; he heard the dry rustling of the papers on the notice board. Somewhere, high in the building, there was a distant sound of a slamming door. It had been very far away and only the relative quietness had allowed Alexander to hear it.

The door of Robert's room opened. Coincidentally, the moon came out of its obscurity.

'Who's there? Is it you, Robert?' The voice was low, almost a whisper.

'No, it isn't.'

The girl did not seem surprised to see Alexander. 'Oh, it's you, I ought to have expected it.' Her voice sounded relieved; it had a sudden confidence to it. She no longer spoke softly.

'The servants must have brought up this bed for me.'

'They've certainly done that.' Her voice was loud and heavy; perhaps she had just woken up from sleep. It was difficult to see any detail of her face in the poor light and it was only possible to make out that she held her head slightly forward and inclined to one side. 'They spent all afternoon messing about on that landing,' she continued. 'First of all Robert and another man – I'm not sure of his name – brought the bed up in pieces; they tried to carry it complete, but the stairs were too narrow and they had to dismantle the thing in the courtyard. Then Mrs Killinger came up and supervised the making of the bed. Mrs Farrard managed to have a row with one of the new women; that was quite a scene. There was a

138

good deal of talk about you. Apparently (so they said) you had borrowed some money. I couldn't believe that at first; you seemed much too cautious to get into debt with them, but they insisted that it was true.'

'I did borrow some money from them.'

'Oh! Then it was true! Didn't you stop to think how unwise it was? Besides, they'll never keep it a secret. They talk about these things and discuss them all the time; they hold nothing in confidence.'

'I was advised to borrow money.' He looked at her and saw her expression. 'Mr Tompkins advised me.'

She looked behind her, towards that open door of the room. 'I can't say anything about that. You obviously had to judge things yourself.'

Alexander said nothing.

'It must have been a difficult decision, to borrow money from the servants. They gossip amongst themselves and impute all kinds of improbabilities to you.' She paused. 'Someone said that you had been to see Mr Sleight.'

'That's my own business.'

The girl laughed; not out of spite, but rather out of a fellow feeling which came from seeing another's actions pursuing a course which results in nothing. 'How did you find his name?'

'It was more or less by chance. I happened to meet Mr Mause; he said that Sleight was a member of the Jacksonian Club, whatever that is.'

'Do you trust Mr Mause's judgement?'

'I don't know him. I've only met him twice.' He lapsed into silence. 'What is the Jacksonian Club?' he asked, suddenly, as though the question had just come to his mind.

The girl made a vague gesture, a shrug of the shoulders which indicated nothing. 'I don't know. They don't talk about their own affairs very much. I've had the impression that the Jacksonian Club was a society for merchants and traders; I don't know. Mr Mause is a member. The town's a difficult town to understand if you have no business interests.' She altered her stance and leaned against the door-jamb. 'What has your day been like? Did you have any success?'

'I don't know what to think. No, it wasn't successful. It was very tiring. I didn't, at the root of it all, trust Mr Sleight and I think that that may have affected what I set out to do; I noticed him looking at me as though he was wondering why I wasn't forthright. He never mentioned anything about it, of course, but I think he knew that, despite what I said, I didn't trust him. It's not strange if you look at it in the way that I did.' He smiled slightly. 'I don't trust him now. He was too slick, too businesslike. What is more I think he was blind to his own problems.'

'You said last night that you would help me.'

'I will. I intend to. First of all, though, I must sort out my own position; I want to know what's happening before I can plan anything, let alone do anything.'

'But you're in debt, now. They'll hardly let you go now that you owe them money. Before, they were examining you out of curiosity; now they have a definite purpose in watching what you do.' She spoke rapidly. Her voice was low and breathless. 'I've avoided debt. It's easier for a woman, and I think I have done as well as I could. Robert gives me enough money for my day to day needs. He's good like that. He never asks me where it goes. I just have to talk to him when he's been drinking: he's very good natured when he comes back after a good evening. I've even been able to save a little; but then I've been saving for both of us because it's quite possible that Robert will want to move out and do something different; he admits quite honestly that he doesn't intend to be a servant all his life. It'll require some savings, that will. As for being in debt, I would be ashamed to think of it.'

'So you aren't going to leave this house?'

'Not yet. Not until Robert decides that it's time for a change. Perhaps I misled you a little when we were talking last night. These are all important things to think about and one has to discuss all the possibilities. As for you, you have got yourself into debt, and you don't even

140

seem to be ashamed of it. Perhaps you don't know the stigma of what it's like to be in debt here. Word passes very swiftly, you know. The servants don't spare you. Because of their own position they take a malicious delight in bringing down people they think are acting above themselves.'

Alexander was aware of the incongruity of the situation. 'I've never pretended to be anyone different from the person I am.'

'I never said you were; I was only saying what could happen. As it is, they were talking of nothing but your financial state. The actual sum of the loan was mentioned, and the high rate of interest which they had squeezed out of you. They expressed their surprise that you hadn't remonstrated about that high interest rate; one of them said that it might indicate that you had no intention of paying the money back. So you can see how quickly the rumours go against you. They even speculated on how much more you might have to borrow.

'It was all talked about. One of them mentioned Mr Sleight and said that he was reputed for his ability to waste his clients' time by making trivia appear to be of great importance. They talk about these things very seriously; there's not a trace of flippancy in their gossip. And you, a debtor, say that you can help me!'

'A debt like mine isn't as important a thing as you make out,' said Alexander. 'It was a transaction. There was nothing underhand about it.'

'You only prove your ignorance by saying that.' She paused. 'Any debt which the servants know about is a very important thing; nothing makes conversation for them as much as a debt, particularly one where they are the creditors.' She stopped talking and it was difficult to tell whether she had tired of that subject or tired of the whole conversation. 'I'm a newcomer here,' she said, suddenly, 'so perhaps I'm making generalizations about things I don't fully understand. There was some truth in your remark when you said that I didn't know whether I wanted to leave or to stay. Your attitudes change when you've been here for some time, they say, and all that you are certain about is that you have no wish to go back. I'm not speaking only from personal experience; I've listened to many people who wanted to talk, though I've taken everything with a pinch of salt. I wonder, sometimes, why I should feel strongly about something I've given up trying to understand; at times I think I'm being foolish, and perhaps reading too much into the situation; perhaps that's why I respect Robert and why I now love him. I do love him. He sees things more confidently; he's solid and unassuming and he has the gift of being able to batter his way through all kinds of impossible situations without realizing what he's doing. He's adept at living in the servants' world without making any effort and therefore any decision or compromise, and he can communicate that security.

'When he's away I think all kinds of abstract things. It's crossed my mind that when I was in the city I took the world for granted in the same way in which Robert takes his world here for granted. There's not much to choose between the two worlds, if you think about it; they're both places, after all, and nothing more. Very little differs; perhaps the emphasis has changed a little and perhaps the standards are not the same.'

Alexander was aware that he had nearly fallen asleep while she had been speaking. 'Why did they put this bed here? Why are they concerned for me?' he asked, inconsequentially.

'It's not so much a matter of their wanting to help you,' said the girl in a resigned way. 'They want to see their money back.'

She stood, leaning against the moulding of the door. Alexander, almost asleep, sat in bed. The wind flowed down the stairs and across the moonlit landing. The ticking of the clock which stood in the hall below was audible; in the quietness of the night there was the impression that its sound had grown louder.

'Do you know Mr Tompkins?' asked Alexander.

'Mr Tompkins?'

Alexander leaned forward. He seemed reluctant to speak. 'He has a room at the front of the house, overlooking the town.'

'Yes, I think I know him. I know who you mean, though perhaps by a different name. I've heard that he answers to any name he's called; he's unlike the servants in that.' She looked at her wrist as though to tell the time, but her action had only been a gesture; she had no watch. 'What's the time?'

'Five, at a guess.'

'It must have gone that. It's very late. I wonder where Robert is?'

'Doesn't he tell you when he's coming back?'

'No, he doesn't. I wouldn't have it any other way; you can never trust what he says.' And then she said something which surprised Alexander; it surprised him out of his tiredness. 'I've wondered while I've been listening to you whether you don't regard the servants as adversaries.'

'They are adversaries.'

'Why should you think that? It's strange. I've never thought of looking at them in that light. Perhaps you're not wrong; at least if you approach them as adversaries it puts you on your guard. Another thing I've noticed – and I may be wrong; perhaps it's just a result of thinking of them as being against you – is that you look at them as though they were coordinated against you. That isn't true. They live in their own world and they are forever supporting and deceiving each other all the time.' She stood in thought; she had reached a sudden conclusion. 'You think about things in a very odd way, but I wonder if you aren't right. There is something in common between them, though it's difficult to know what makes them act together. Perhaps you only realize that something links them when you try to take advantage of the fact that they seem to be so rarely coordinated.'

'I'm not sure that it's really important.'

143

'Perhaps not for you. My relations with Robert makes me different.'

'One thing that stood out during my visit to Mr Tompkins was that he seemed to be above the struggles of the servants.'

The girl smiled because of an inner preoccupation. 'You think they struggle, do you? No, not really. Only on the surface. When they are alone they indulge in all kinds of petty quarrels – I've many times found myself unobserved in a corner of the servants' hall, in a position to listen to what they were saying – but they change. They present a very unified front when they are questioned or challenged by a visitor. If you could only listen to the difference between them speaking amongst themselves and speaking to a visitor! Yesterday I heard you ask one of them for a set of directions for something. "An official Course of Instruction" you called it. I heard the servant's reply. Of course, he gave the stock reply which any servant would have given; you might not have recognized that it was a stock reply because you haven't been here very long, though a person who was a judge of people might have had some insight. Perhaps you were misled by its apparent timeliness. The one truth is that his reply was a stock reply; he gave you a catechist's response. Any other servant would have answered in the same way. None of them would have understood what you meant.'

'I remember asking the question. I had no idea that I had been overheard.'

'It wasn't done on purpose,' said the girl, disliking the implication. 'I don't want to listen to visitors' questions. They are so predictable that they become dispiriting when you've heard them all before; besides, they are the questions that I would have asked if I thought I might get some sensible reply, but the servants have answers to all those generalities. Anyway, even if I hadn't happened to overhear you – and you were speaking in a loud voice as though to a foreigner – I should have been told, or should have overheard one of them telling

144

another. They can't keep a confidence. I don't know why that is, except that it might be because they wish to forewarn their colleagues of what kind of questions a particular visitor had asked and might be expected to ask again. The very fact that a stock reply was given shows that the question was not understood. To ask a servant a specific question serves only to bewilder him, or it would do had it not been repeated so many times that he no longer thought about it before giving a stock answer in a parrot-fashion way. The answers to the expected questions are all set down in a phrase book which all the servants carry.'

'A phrase book? What do you mean?'

'Haven't you seen one?'

'No, I haven't.'

'Don't sound so surprised. You might have expected something of the kind; how else do you think they can answer questions which don't make any sense to them? Robert has several of them. They issue new editions to all the servants every year; that's probably why one finds so many old ones thrown away in odd corners.'

Alexander had suddenly become very sleepy and his eyes closed against his will. He remembered that he had once, for a few minutes, perhaps while he had been in Mr Sleight's back room, nursed the suspicion that there had been some artefact of speech which had conditioned the way in which the servants had replied to his questions. He had dismissed the idea; it had seemed so improbable that he had wondered why he had thought of it. 'Are you serious when you say that they speak a different language? It all seems so unreasonable! Besides, I'm tired. You're speaking like Mr Tompkins; you could have borrowed his words. You're obviously voicing someone else's thoughts.'

'What if I am? I owe so much to other people and especially to Mr Tompkins. I've found out from experience that he is very much in touch with the things which happen in the house; it's strange, because he never seems to leave his room. He never sees the servants;

145

some of them think that he no longer lives in the house. Some of them think of him as a fictitious person invented by the visitors for their support. It's when they get talking about things like this that they are difficult to understand; it's then that one realizes that they mean something very different from what they say. It's not that they are being dishonest; far from it.'

'I must wash before I sleep,' said Alexander. The ticking of the clock below had grown yet louder and he thought he could hear quick echoes to its beat. 'I'm tired.'

'Of course you are!' She seemed surprised that he had delayed going to bed for so long. 'You'll find a towel at the end of the bed-rail, and beyond this landing,' she pointed to a narrow panelled door, 'there's a short corridor which leads to a bathroom. I think they must have put some soap out for you. I remember Mrs Killinger shouting at one of the men to see to it.'

Alexander climbed out of bed. He took the towel and, without saying anything he walked to the narrow door. A sudden thought arrested him and he stood half in and half out of the dark corridor. 'Were you being honest when you were talking about the servants?'

'About what, in particular?'

'When you implied that everything the servants have told me has been in the nature of a stock preparation? It's quite true that they do sometimes speak oddly, as though from a phrase book, as though making a recitation . . . but you can't say that they speak a different language just because of that.'

'Of course they speak the same language! That's partly where the trouble lies; they use the same language to describe different things, different experiences, different beliefs and ambitions. That's why it's so easy to misunderstand them. To them we are both foreign, and obviously so. Because they do speak the same language it's easy for us to fall into the trap of believing that they think in much the same way as ourselves.

'They are not adversaries; they go out of their way to

help you. Haven't I just told you that they go to the bother of equipping themselves with phrase books specifically for the purpose of answering visitors' questions? They have no need to do that as far as I can tell. I'm only saying what I feel is true.'

Alexander considered this. 'They have a strange way of being helpful,' he said.

'No; you can't impute all the blame to them. Even the most helpful person can't always avoid being clumsy on occasion. The toneless rendition of a stock phrase, given in order to answer a question, may sound wooden and even disorientated, but for all that the question gets an answer.' She looked back into the room.

'Can you find me one of these books?'

'Haven't I just said that I will? I'll give it you in the morning.'

Alexander felt a sense of urgency which he could not begin to explain. The idea of a standard phrase book must be either a metaphor or a fabrication the meaning of which was to illustrate a spurious point. 'They really exist, these books?'

'Of course they do. They are thin, limp books with grey covers. As I was saying, there are several old ones in Robert's room.'

'You couldn't get one for me now, could you?'

He had expected her to be impatient, but she was not; she ran towards him and for a moment it seemed that she might be about to clamber over the bed in order to stand by him; she smiled a spontaneous smile which showed nothing but good nature. 'You hesitate over nothing, do you!' She looked at him with pleasure and friendliness. 'I admire you for that; you obviously know your own mind. It's good to be suspicious; it defends you against apathy. And it's nice for me not to become encumbered with your confidences. Here ...' She looked over the handrail and down the stairs. 'I'll get you one from a room on the floor below. I think I can put my hand on it. That room's never used. I'd better not take one of Robert's; he would never notice, but there's a

147

chance that the cleaner might. I'll put it on your bed where you'll find it when you come out of the bathroom, but you won't be able to read it tonight; there's no light on this landing. One last thing; don't let the servants see you reading it.' She squeezed herself between the bed-head and the stair-rail and, turning once more to smile at him, she made her way quickly and silently down the stairs.

When Alexander returned from the bathroom he saw, in the vague moonlight, the shape of the book which lay on the bed. He picked it up. He judged from its feel that it had been well used. It was limp and too large to fit into a pocket; an awkward size and surely unsuited to a phrase book. There were no more than twenty or thirty pages in it. For all that he was able to make of it it might have been a book of mathematical tables.

Although he had been told that there was no light on this landing he looked automatically for a switch; he found one and turned it on. Lights came on all the way up and down the staircase, in the hall below and on the landing itself.

'They must have repaired them,' said the girl. 'Did you find the book?'

'Yes, I did.'

She stood as she had done before, leaning against the moulding of the door frame. She seemed very wakeful. Alexander wondered when she found time to sleep.

'Will this . . .' and he held up the book in his right hand '. . . tell me anything about the letter?'

'I doubt if it'll tell you anything you couldn't find out from Mr Tompkins,' she said. 'I hope it's of use to you. You seemed to be eager enough to see a copy.'

'You say that there are several editions.'

'Yes. That one's an old edition. They don't change much, though, and often you can only tell how old a book is by looking at the type. That changes from year to year. I'll leave that book with you. I don't know what you'll make of it; some of it's very odd. It's full of overstatement, but perhaps that's only because it is intended for the servants' use. The text itself reads like a catechism: question, answer and explanation. The questions are simple, very much like the questions you have asked yourself. The answers, too, don't take much following, even though they are oblique; they are more often than not vague generalities which prompt you to ask further questions. One often has the impression that they are phrased that way on purpose. An important question always seems to lead to a vague answer which, in its turn, invites another but much less important question; there's a kind of reaction which ends up with an answer which is so self-obvious that the questioner comes to regard himself and his original question as being foolish.

'But – and this is an interesting thing – the third part of the catechism, the explanations, give the lie to the purpose behind the whole book. The phrase book is written for servants by servants.'

Alexander, who had been sitting at the edge of the bed looking at his two hands as they lay clasped together, raised his glance and saw the bareness of the landing and the staircase as though for the first time. He saw the peeling paint and the cracks and the weeping knots in the unseasoned woodwork. He saw the sagging wires and the rows of electrical conduits. It was an unpleasant thought to consider that one might have to spend an indeterminate time living in such surroundings. He looked up at the girl. Most of what she had said had been quite above his head. 'How long have you been here?' he asked.

'Why does that matter?'

'It doesn't matter. I'd like to know.'

'I won't tell you that. It's not that I don't trust you; far from it. But after one has been here for some time one is very naturally reticent about giving anything away. Besides, if I answered you it wouldn't mean very much. People often lie about how long they have been here. You wouldn't know if I were telling the truth or not.'

'Have it your own way. It's not worth arguing over.' He had been looking over the hand-rail and had noticed that the treads of the stairs were worn down. He had seen stairs worn into such hollows in an old collegiate building. Perhaps these stairs were older than they looked, or perhaps they received heavy traffic, or perhaps they had been made of poor materials. 'You've been talkative tonight. What prompted that?'

She did not smile at the attempt at humour in the underhand question. 'What time is it?' she asked.

'I don't know. It's getting light.'

They both looked at the landing window. A moment ago it had been a rectangle of blackness; now it was suffused with an uncertain indigo.

The light grew quickly. The indigo became blue-grey and the scene from the window began to take on structure. The buildings beyond and below appeared indistinctly out of the night.

The sudden rapidity of the dawn revealed roof after roof; slate, tile, copper or lead sheathed, all without any architectural uniformity. Some of the roofs were pitched steeply; some were vast expanses of asphalt or asbestos. The pots of high chimneys were beginning to smoke.

On the landing the sound of the clock was now inaudible against the sound of the birds. The notices on the baize board ceased to be uncertain shapes and the print upon them was becoming distinct.

'I don't suppose Robert will come now,' said the girl prosaically, making a statement to herself. 'I think I'll go, now.' She went back into the room and closed the door quietly behind her.

Distantly a bell tolled and, shortly afterwards, a telephone rang unanswered in a room in a building across the courtyard.

Alexander turned off the unnecessary light.

The bedstead must have been very much in the way of anyone descending the stairs for it occupied most of the floor area of the landing. Alexander, half asleep, was distantly aware of creaking stair-treads and heavy foot-falls in the corridor above. Once he awoke to find that someone, half drugged with sleep, was climbing over his bed to reach the staircase. Once the bed was violently jolted as though someone had been running precipitately down the stairs from the very top of the building and had not seen the bed until about to collide with it.

The sounds grew less. The doors banged more infrequently and the noise of running feet might never have occurred except as a dream. The building was in a state of undisturbed day-time silence and motes of dust hung in the shaft of light which crossed the landing from the window.

Alexander woke; the elevation of the sun allowed him some indication of the time. He reached under the pillow for the facsimile of the letter and for the phrase book. Both were there. He reached for the book and saw that the cover had no writing on it. He opened the book and saw that there was neither preface nor title; the minute grey print started at the top of the first of the coarse yellow pages and continued with no interruption until half way down the last page. The first impression that the book gave was that it was a portion of print taken *en bloc* from a larger work. The minuteness of the print and the coarseness of the paper made it difficult to read even before the sense was apprehended. He turned back to the first page and began to read, awkwardly, screwing up his eyes, but he had hardly begun before he looked up. A sound had distracted him; a slight noise, hardly perceptible.

The tall servant was sitting on the end of the bed. He had turned his head to look out of the window. The movement of his neck on his starched collar had made that slight sound.

He sat motionlessly. His breathing was imperceptible. His face, as far as could be seen from his oblique profile, had an expressionless immobility. It was impossible to tell what he was thinking about. It was clear that he knew that Alexander was awake and watching him;

indeed, it would have been improbable to suppose that he was unaware of anything that happened on the landing; he had an air of observant watchfulness, an impression heightened by his very silence. But for all that he stared out of the window. Alexander wondered whether his orders were more complicated than usual. It crossed his mind that the servant would make no direct approach until Alexander signified that he was aware of his presence.

Perhaps out of fear Alexander ignored him. He tried feigning sleep but he could not do this. Apart from the ridiculous situation he was now in he was uncomfortable; the shoulder he was leaning on ached and his arm was growing stiff. He clenched and unclenched his fist, watching the action of the tendons of his wrist. He did not know how to break the silence but he had the urge to get out of the tall servant's presence; he could stand it no longer. He got out of bed hurriedly and put a towel round his waist. He went through the door which led to the passage and the bathroom and lavatory. As he closed the passage door behind him he saw the servant still sitting, motionless, staring out of the window. For the first time he saw that he wore a different suit, a formal black suit that seemed to have had little wear. Alexander closed the door and shut himself in the bathroom. He ran the water and washed himself. He shaved with the razor he had found last night; the familiarity of the action was a kind of easy solace.

It was inevitable that he would have to unlock the door and face the servant again, and it seemed pointless to postpone the moment. He opened the door and walked to the bed. He dressed himself quickly and prepared to walk down the stairs. He pushed his way past the bed and grasped the stair-rail.

'Wait.'

Alexander turned; the servant had stood and was now looking down at him. 'There's no point in my waiting,' said Alexander, surprised at the gasping way he said this, aware of the unexpected and hesitant breathlessness of his own enunciation.

'I didn't hear what you said. I have been asked to tell you that Mr Tompkins would like to see you.' He began to walk down the stairs, Alexander retreating before him.

'There's no need for me to see him.'

'Why can't you be reasonable?' For the first time the servant's face showed some emotion. 'What's the matter with you this morning?'

'You disturbed me with your silence.' Alexander was less afraid of him now that he had spoken.

'What do you mean? I was waiting for you to wake; I could hardly have been more considerate. I couldn't have done much more. What do you expect me to do?' He looked down. 'I see that you are holding one of those phrase books.'   .

'Someone lent it to me. What's wrong with that?'

The tall man looked at him with a certain amount of perplexity. 'There's nothing wrong. Only that that phrase book will do you no good.'

They stood together in the hall. An observer might have mistaken them for two men talking on equal terms, but it certainly did not seem like that to Alexander. 'I was told that it might give me some insight into what happens in this house.'

'Do you think so? Do you really think so?' He looked at Alexander as though the latter had said something cleverly apposite but fundamentally untrue. 'Let me have a look at it.' He reached out for it and when it was passed to him he immediately opened it. 'I have never understood why they print new editions,' he said. 'In the past I have had to read many editions, and I can't remember seeing any substantial changes in the text; they are too afraid to alter the text. It is a confusion of words, a pile of arguments which have to do with controversies long dead. I suppose it would be of interest to an historian.' He handed the book back. 'I have met people in this house who for some reason have come to rely on it. They are able to quote it, word for word as though it had an oracular importance.

'Perhaps they would be worse off it they didn't have a

153

fundamentalist faith in it. Who can tell? Given an appropriate predicament anyone will clutch at a straw.' He looked at his watch. 'Come on.'

Alexander followed him across the courtyard and through the metal-framed door. The servant led the way down the passage into the dark interior of the old building; he did not look back to see whether the visitor was following him.

The route they were taking was a circuitous one though it seemed that the servant had mapped it out in advance and now held the plan in his head. Many of the corridors and stairways were new to Alexander; others he had seen before, distantly, leaving him wondering where they might lead if followed in their entirety.

'Why are we going this way?' he asked. He saw that the servant was in haste; his quick walk made no concessions to those who might find difficulty in sustaining that rapid pace. 'If there is a need to hurry what stops you taking the more direct way?'

The servant was too far away and ahead to hear him. Alexander began to run, clumsily, aware of the echo of the sound of his own footfalls, until he was almost abreast of the man. 'If there is a need to hurry, what stops you taking a more direct way?' He had the sudden premonition that he was being led into an unknown place – the route was certainly too long and the corridors themselves were too broad and too straight to conform to the confines of the original house – and in his reluctance to continue he felt constrained to speak, as though speech would in some way slow down or modify the pace of the servant's progress. 'I was called here by letter,' he said.

The servant looked at him, saying nothing but inclining his head as though to show that he had heard.

'I understand that you were summoned here by telephone,' continued Alexander.

The servant looked ahead to a vague meeting-place of several corridors and made no comment; his purposeful pace did not alter.

'What's the importance behind these things?'

'If you wish to burden me by talking about your letter I can't stop you,' said the servant, his voice suggesting that even he was out of breath. 'And you can keep any conjecture about a telephone call which I may or may not have received to yourself. These things are private. None of us is here to talk about himself. You have to be circumspect in what you say and in what you do. One of the reasons why we are taking this way is for the benefit of any onlookers: can't you see that I'm trying to prevent you from getting the reputation of being a man of habit?'

Despite his rapid pace his manner had become preoccupied and thoughtful. He seemed to relent of what he had said. For the first time he paused. They stood in a passage which had frequent doors to the right and a line of empty benches to the left. 'You can tell me about your letter, if you like, but I don't think I can be of any help. Your letter arrived; your letter and your state of mind accided at the same time, in the way all these messages do. There's not much more to be said than that; you have to accept it. The more you search for a reason the more you enmesh yourself in speculation; it's a fruitless task and I don't believe that you can reach a satisfactory outcome unless you are prepared to support your speculation by means of small tricks of personal dishonesty. Occasionally you meet those who think they have discovered the purpose of the message: it's usually the case that the ones with the poorest and crudest arguments are the very ones who shout out that they have the greatest right to communicate their conclusions; their proclamations only emphasize their rigidity of outlook. Like everyone else they grow old. There is no talk of reason when the night fevers come and the cot-sides are put in place.' His voice was quiet; he had spoken without showing any particular emotion, in the manner of someone who has discovered something to be true a long time ago, and who, in his subsequent experiences, has found no cause to change his mind.

3

Mr Tompkins stood at the window of his room, staring downwards at the town. Superficially his stare was the incurious stare of a bored man. He had his hands in his pockets where they jangled keys; the sound was at variance with his manner, which, below the superficial boredom, was uneasy. It was difficult to tell what he was looking at.

'Why are you here?'

'I was told that you wished to see me.'

'Yes, that was true.' He gave very little away as he spoke the words. 'I thought you might wish to show me the reconstruction of your letter.'

Alexander hesitated, though the letter was in his hands. 'I have the facsimile here. It was drawn up as you suggested.' As he held out the letter he knew that he was dissatisfied with the work which he had put into it. Although he was still unsure as to whether the original letter was of any importance, he was aware that the difference between the original and the reconstruction might have a significance greater than he had supposed. The thought was unpleasant because it cast doubts on his ability to recall the past or to make any surmise as to what might happen in the days ahead; if a reappraisal of an unimportant thing was to prove so unsatisfactory, what would happen in the future? He held out the letter and his hesitancy grew.

Mr Tompkins took the letter from him and read it. His manner was scarcely less anxious than Alexander's own. 'I see that you've put a lot of work into this. It is

156

drawn up in the manner one might have suggested. It must have taken time; you've spared nothing.'

'I'm afraid I had little trust in the agent who copied it. I had little trust then and I have none now. I don't know how much this letter represents the original.'

He still looked at the letter. 'Yesterday you told me that your letter was of no importance. Now you are anxious for my comment even on a copy of it.' He took his time. 'Perhaps you kept your scribe on too tight a rein while you employed him.'

'What do you mean by that?'

'Perhaps you did not allow him the freedom to show you the whole range of the tools of his trade.' Mr Tompkins said nothing for a while; when he next spoke it was as if something new had entered his mind. 'How are you finding the course?'

'The official course?'

Mr Tompkins turned to him. 'Yes, if you like. The official course. I notice that you lay emphasis on the word "official". Do you know what it means?'

'Of course I do. I wouldn't use the word if I didn't know what it meant.'

'I don't think that's true. I notice that you are carrying what they call a phrase book, though it is not so much a phrase book as a dictionary of current language usage. Have you looked up the word in that? No; I can see that you have not. I can tell you now that the word "official" occupies several pages, though to be truthful those pages deal with rare uses and archaisms that have no place any longer. The word itself means little, but the little that it does mean shows that you can't use the word indiscriminately, as though you were plucking it from the air to say what you want. In the words of the dictionary its use must depend on its context: adopted in a certain way it means one thing; used in another way it has a different meaning. You can use that single word in any way you wish, provided you use it in the correct context. The claim of the dictionary is simple despite the many wasted pages. "A course of action may be considered official if it adheres to the principles of current thinking." Does that help you? I know it wouldn't help me. I've no idea what the principles of current thinking are, as laid down by those who assume the authority to state dicta like that. I've no idea of the identity of these people who assume authority and I mistrust their motives. I dislike that book. It's difficult to know what to think; I notice that you use the word as a qualifying adjective to add weight to what you say; you use it innocently, perhaps not knowing what it means. Beyond this room I don't think it would be understood in that sense.'

'How long have you been here?' asked Alexander.

'I've been here for four years,' said Mr Tompkins prosaically. 'I was in this house for some time before that. This room, as I think I once told you, belonged to a man who was a collector of things. He encouraged visitors; he must have had a philanthropic turn of mind. I must admit to you that I had no idea what I was letting myself in for when I took this room.' He put his hands together and locked his attenuated fingers. 'I'll open the window. The room needs airing.' He pulled down the sash with a single brisk movement. Immediately the sounds of the town below were audible. The incoming wind disturbed his hair. 'I had no idea what my task would turn out to be. I came here for peace but it was impossible to find it. At first I had no wish to help those who found their way here. Who was I to presume to help them? What was my advice worth? Most of them were so preoccupied with whatever it was that was worrying them that they seized on what I said without regard for its worth. More than that; because of the intensity of their search and their fear they would twist anything I said to them. I did not want to be an oracle. I didn't want to advise people who only heard what they wished to hear, particularly when that wish was for precipitate action towards an unthought end.

'I was forced to learn a great deal. Do you remember that I told you about the telephone call of the man who brought you here this morning? He is a circumspect

158

man. Most of them are not. They want me to alter the circumstances in which they find themselves; they want a kind of martyrdom for all that they have undergone; their wish is a thing of the moment, burning hot and stoked by anxiety. Who did they think I was when they sought me? Why do they expect me to fulfil the latest wish of a moment? Why do they come to me when they know more about the extremity of their circumstances than I? Why do they come to me?'

Through the open window, down below them and about a half a mile away, a pile-driver started. The slow concussions re-echoed across the valley .

'What are they building?' asked Alexander.

'I'm told it's another annexe,' said Mr Tompkins. 'They are building to a plan, so the visitors tell me.'

He looked out of the window and Alexander, following his gaze, saw that one side of the further hill was mutilated by excavated terraces. 'The bribes are only the simplest kind of corruption,' said Mr Tompkins, leaving it unclear as to whether he was talking about the valley or the events within the house. 'There's nothing one can do about it.' He closed the window and the sound of the outer noise was cut off.

Alexander wondered why he had not seen the new building work before; yesterday the valley had seemed to be no more than a peaceful provincial place, holding between its hills a town, a variegation of sudden altering perspectives which he might have seen from the window of a train when he was travelling as a boy at the start of the school holidays.

'If I were you,' said Mr Tompkins, 'I would let things continue in their course. You might be short of money, but if that is the case then you must use my card and offer what authority I have as security; it isn't much, but then you are not in need of much. The tendency here is to exaggerate small things, magnifying them beyond proportion, using them as a kind of concealing cloak. Your requirements are insignificant. Put things into perspective and use my card to get what you want.' He looked

159

back at the window. 'I sound like a fool who ought to have learned by experience. You should ignore me. You look unwell and I don't know why you've listened to me with such patience.'

That afternoon Alexander happened to be standing in the hall of the house. He had nothing to do and he did not wish to invent a task. The day had become overcast and it was raining and each window allowed a tearful prospect of either the moor or the valley. The rain pattered on the roofs and was audibly swallowed by the down-pipes and the drains. It was a dark day but the lights had not yet been switched on.

'Where are you going?' He did not recognize the voice at first; the figure was shadowy and difficult to make out. 'Don't pretend you don't recognize me.'

Alexander peered along the length of the corridor and saw Robert walking towards him.

'Where are you going?' Robert asked again.

'Nowhere.' He saw that Robert carried a suitcase; he was breathing hard as though he had run up several flights of stairs.

'Apsleigh's secretary told me to give you this,' said Robert. 'I don't know what is in it, but I suspect it may be a change of clothes.'

'Why?'

'I suppose he thought it would do, considering your original case was mislaid somewhere in the house.' He paused. 'Have you got a moment?'

'Certainly.'

'Come into the kitchen, then, and sign for this case. You'd better examine its contents and make sure that you know what you are signing.' Without waiting he led the way to the kitchen.

In the kitchen Mrs Killinger and Mr Apsleigh's assistant were sitting at the scrubbed table drinking from small sherry glasses. They both looked upward as the door opened; for a moment it seemed that they might stand; they both made movements which suggested that they might be about to stand and when neither of them did it seemed slightly surprising: they had mirrored each other's actions without even glancing at each other. They both turned and looked at Robert and Alexander. Neither of them said anything.

Robert put the case down and ignored Alexander; he stared at the two sitting servants. 'Don't I get a glass?' His voice had resumed its usual abruptness.

Mrs Killinger tilted her head and glanced momentarily at Alexander. 'It would mean leaving the visitor out. You know that it is prohibited for a visitor to consume any of the victuals provided by the house. Perhaps it would be more polite if you forewent your glass in order to keep him company.' She spoke regretfully but as though voicing a rule.

'Well, give us both a drink then. It won't kill you to break a rule for once.' Robert put one of his feet on the seat of a chair and rested his forearm on his knee. He looked across at Mrs Killinger. Unexpectedly, he winked. 'No?'

'I can't, Robert. Don't ask me to. The breaking of a rule always necessitates a lie, and I've told too many lies on his behalf already.'

'I was only asking for a drink. You can't leave him out.'

'I'm sorry, but it is not possible.'

'We all break rules when it suits us. You do; you make no bones about it. You leave early when you go down to the church on Tuesdays to do whatever you do there.'

'That's not the point at issue. Officially speaking, the church is part of the house.'

Robert straightened himself and removed his foot from the seat of the chair. He turned to Alexander. 'We'll go down to the town and have a drink there. Will that suit you? It'll do us both good to get out.' His glance fell on the case and he looked at it as though perhaps wondering what was in it. 'Come on. You can look at that case later.'

The invitation was so unexpected that Alexander agreed to go, but there was a reluctance in his manner.

'What's the matter? Are you afraid about your course or something like that?'

'No; I have no money.'

Robert smiled. 'Is that what you're concerned about? I never asked you if you had any money; I asked you if you'd like to come for a drink. Something better than Mrs Killinger's sherry.'

Mrs Killinger had reverted back to her conversation with Mr Apsleigh's assistant, but it was clear that she was trying to overhear what Robert was saying.

One of the bells began to ring. Robert, who had been walking to the door, ignored it; he did not even alter his pace. Mrs Killinger, interrupted in what she was saying, raised her voice which remained raised even when the bell had stopped.

Alexander closed the kitchen door; Robert had already walked a long way up the corridor and now stood, looking back. Alexander ran to catch him up. 'What was that bell?'

'Not one of the important ones; you can tell that from the way it is rung.' He seemed disinterested in the bell.

'Do you know then who is ringing it?'

'No; how could I? I happen to recognize it as the front door bell. No one of any importance goes to the front door; it takes so long to get in, because no one is in a hurry to answer it. In fact, none of the servants will bother to answer it at all nowadays except Mrs Killinger, who will go to open the door when the noise of the bell becomes too loud for her to talk above it. Some of the others will answer it out of a sense of pity. That's about all.'

The bell continued to ring.

'Are we leaving by the front door?' asked Alexander.

Robert shook his head. 'There's a servants' door that leads directly into the garden.' He winked. 'According to Mrs Killinger only servants are supposed to have the right to use it, so don't go telling her that I've taken you through it.'

They turned a corner in the monotonous corridor.

Ahead of them the new section of passage was filled with brilliant daylight which entered from a glazed double door. Outside, the garden was radiant with a dappled light which fell from a break in the clouds. The air was fresh from the recent rain and it was possible to see for many miles across the plain.

Perhaps it was only at times like this that the unusual position of the house was fully realized; away to the southwest, down on the plain, the storm continued; from the house the bases of the anvil clouds seemed to be surprisingly close to the flat fields of the chequered landscape; the curtains of distant rain wheeled as they fell with a remote and silent slowness.

By contrast with the wandering expanse of the house the front garden was small, though it was well protected by trees; the sudden sunlight had put warmth in the air. The sound of the thunder from the distant storm had a regular and artificial quality to it which made it resemble the brief and dull concussions of quarry blasting.

Robert left the door ajar. Now that he was in the garden he was in no hurry to continue; he stood, his hands on his hips, looking down into the valley. 'Elizabeth was telling me about you,' he said, making a statement. 'She seemed to think that you'd have a bad time in the house. I said that I didn't know how she could tell that, but she said it was intuition.'

'What did she mean by "a bad time"?'

'Unhappiness,' said Robert unexpectedly. 'She thought that you would have difficulty in conforming to the life expected of you as a servant; one has to conform to live harmoniously.' He began to walk down the sunlit lawn.

'She may have misunderstood you,' said Robert, after some minutes of silence. 'I sometimes think that she's unsure in her own mind about this course of instruction thing that you've been telling her about; according to her you didn't make it clear whether it is real or whether it is something which you were forced to invent; she says that she suspects that you don't know the answer to that

163

yourself. Perhaps I shouldn't have mentioned the subject; I wouldn't have done so if it hadn't made an impression on Elizabeth. It's out of place for me to speak; it's nothing to do with me.'

'The letter stated the existence of the course; it stated it with emphasis. It was certainly not invented by myself.'

'That's nothing to do with me.' Robert seemed embarrassed. 'Though whenever you mention this course you speak as though it were a series of formal lectures. You seem definite about that, even though you must have considered the other meanings of the word.'

Alexander had had the idea of the 'official course' fixed in his head; when he had first arrived at the house he had expected, at any moment, for the unreasonable confusion over his arrival to be clarified; he had expected to be given the full curriculum of the course, the titles of the lectures and the seminars, the names of the speakers. Although, latterly, he had grown sceptical of its existence, the thought that he might have gravely misinterpreted the word had not occurred to him. This new-found need for an alteration in his understanding of the letter made him instantly aware of the utter pointlessness of his trivializing over unimportant detail with Mr Sleight. The ambiguity, unseen until now, perplexed him because he wondered what else he had missed. He was profoundly sorry that he no longer had the original letter with him. 'I can take nothing at face value!' he said, aloud.

'It's nothing to do with me,' said Robert again. 'But you often have to take things as they appear to you; at face value as you would say.' He looked back towards the house. 'Some people invent complexities for the sake of it. Mrs Killinger does that; you've seen for yourself how she goes on about the difference between a visitor and a servant; it's so intense, sometimes, that you really think that she believes there is a difference. There is no difference and there is no use in pretending there is. That's where Mrs Killinger goes wrong. It's not so much that she has to invent principles by which to live, but that she must invent points of comparison.'

They walked down the road to the town in silence. The row of houses behind them looked greyly indifferent. Viewed from the road, the house itself was small; its facade was featureless and its outlines were indistinct.

Although he was given neither encouragement nor discouragement Alexander continued to live in the house. He was given a room and duties to carry out. 'One must put up with this life as a temporary measure,' he said to himself more than once. He determined to adapt himself to live in this house until he could attain a clear view of what he should or should not do. Besides, it would have been difficult for him to return to the city; his previous life was more of a desiccated shadow than it had seemed while he had lived it and any wish to return was difficult to imagine.

Once he had accepted that the hierarchy of the servants was an artificial structure, created in the past almost arbitrarily for the sake of a forgotten expediency, he managed to make his way. His own impermanent position seemed scarcely less secure than that of many of the servants.

'You are as secure as you feel yourself to be,' he was told. 'Any threatening event is imaginary until it occurs. Wait until you are a servant. You will know what it means then, even though nothing will seem to have altered. When you are a servant you'll have to make a choice. Some of them are resilient enough to admit that there may be changes in the future; some are more enclosed and envisage an unalterable rule of order which governs their lives and in which they have a part. It is these who make it their own business to concern themselves with the visitors because the visitor, on his arrival here, anticipates some sort of structured order; this anticipation is gratefully pandered to by those servants who wish to project an idea of their own importance in their hierarchy.'

'A servant,' he was told, probably in a cynical moment, 'is only a visitor who no longer bothers to examine himself.'

Alexander found himself wondering how he might approach Mr Tompkins in order to seek his advice.

It was many years before he saw Mr Tompkins again. Elizabeth and Robert had had a child, Alexander had been chosen as the godfather, even though the parents must have known the difficulties which this might cause. Alexander officially became a servant because of the incongruity of his own situation; it would have been impossible for him to assume, as a visitor, a spiritual responsibility for the child.

The official board met and installed him as a servant.

Although he had undertaken his responsibilities at the christening with a sincere sense of duty, he walked listlessly through the town from the church. The day was overcast and the prospect of an afternoon in the house was unpleasant; he had a brief vision of a stretch of dreary corridor which was no particular corridor but a summation of many.

When he arrived back in the house he went to see Mr Tompkins immediately. He knocked at the familiar door at the end of the passage, and then opened it. He began to speak, seeing Mr Tompkins in the room; he was anxious to inform him of his own change of status and to tell him about the christening.

Mr Tompkins stared at him. 'Why are you here?'

'What do you mean?' Alexander found himself affronted by the rapidity of the question, given without any preamble. 'I hope that I am not speaking out of place.' He was aware that he had spoken condescendingly, as though this call on Mr Tompkins had been something of a necessary and polite formality. 'I wasn't aware that I was breaching any matter of protocol,' he said. 'I am sorry if I have.'

'Protocol? What protocol? What are you talking about?' Mr Tompkins stood up suddenly, his expression

166

not critical but anxious. 'Look at yourself. Why are you here?'

Alexander could do no more than to stare back at him.

'How much weight have you lost?' He took a pace towards Alexander but checked himself, as though he were a dog at the end of a running chain. 'You are ill!' He pointed to a wooden chair, perhaps using the action to hide a sudden embarrassment. 'Haven't you seen your own face in a mirror? Sit down.'

'Do I look unwell?' Alexander felt a sense of enervation as he spoke. 'What do you want?' The fact that this visit had gone wrong from the start was of little importance for it was overshadowed by Mr Tompkins' directly communicative anxiety.

'What do I want? What reason have you to ask a question like that?' His voice lost its tension and he shrugged his shoulders as though to excuse in advance the circumlocutions which would come to his lips. He spoke regretfully and uneasily. 'I have always had a sympathy with the weak-minded and the slow; it is easy to see through their guile when they come here. They stand here, pulling at their clothes and fussing over the manner in which they present themselves, as though these things make a difference to the outcome. I can understand them; I have something in common with them.

'But you: you are ill, and yet you seem to think that you can act as though you were at your ease. You aren't like the educated people who come here; you don't try to hide the important things from me. You showed long ago that you had an understanding of what I could offer you: I had mistakenly thought that this might have been the cause of your present visit. I don't understand you.

'I'm foolish. I have seen too much brazen pretence at openness and too much deceitful circuitousness to be able to judge anything with impartiality. Perhaps I am now speaking out of turn; I'm sure that you meant well enough when you came here this afternoon.' He turned to the window; his attitude was one which Alexander had seen many times before. 'I don't get much respite and I have to give way sometimes; perhaps that shows the respect in which I hold you. I have to make up my own standards. I have no course to refer to; I have no longer any course to undertake and sometimes I am uncertain of my own integrity.'

Alexander paused at the door; there seemed to be no point in his staying but he was reluctant to leave without a valediction. 'You said that I looked ill. That concerns me.'

'I said,' murmured Mr Tompkins, without emphasis, ' "You are ill." '

One day Alexander had cause to be in the gardens. He stood in the disused orangery and the shadows of the worm-eaten glazing bars and the dead limbs of the dried trees dappled and camouflaged his face and body. The building faced south and, protected by the mass of the house from the worst of the weather, it had kept most of its glass. It was difficult to know what its purpose was now. Alexander had never been familiar with the gardens and this building, the first of a series of glass-houses, had been unknown to him.

The floor of the orangery was filled with rows of chairs with plywood backs and seats facing in one direction; perhaps the orangery had, at some intermediate stage in its life, been used as a conference hall. However, the chairs had not been used for some time; the winter dampness had caused the glue of many of the plywood seats to deliquesce, allowing the mildewed plies to spring apart. What course might once have been held here? Beside some of the chairs were plastic folders and beside one or two were briefcases, left undisturbed to the mildew. At the head of the orangery was a lectern and a blackboard, while at the other end of the room the barrel of a projector pointed over the seats towards a screen streaked with vertical green stains.

Alexander moved through the system of defunct

green-houses, along alleys where the dried plants were rooted in desiccated pots of earthenware or terracotta on the stone staging, their labels dusty and unreadable. Burst heating pipes, red with rust, sagged from their supports. He walked slowly through the deserted acreage until he could go no further. Here, forced to stop by the brambles which grew as profusely inside as they did outside the glasshouses, he stood and saw the continuation of the line of glass-roofed buildings, enveloped by the thorn-covered stems. Outside, a tall sycamore spread its branches into the still air.

Three old gardeners stood beneath the eaves of an ornamental pavilion. If, as seemed likely, they comprised the entire outdoors staff, it was difficult to see what they could do to keep the wilderness of decaying glasshouses in order. At the moment they were doing nothing more than to stare down the hill where the yellow caterpillar graders were preparing the ground for new buildings. Through the smoke of the demolition fires and beyond the graders an area of ground had been pegged out; further still and foundations were being excavated.

Two tall blocks had been completed. Viewed from the garden side they dwarfed and partially hid the original house with its cluster of outbuildings. They had been designed in a foreign city, built of artificial materials, and they were unsuited to their setting. There was nothing about their angularity or their uncompromising symmetry which suggested that they had anything in common with the local surroundings. There was a stark international facelessness in their proportions: the spirit of their architecture might have been taken from any modern city.

Alexander skirted the new buildings as he returned to the house. He stood beneath the familiar porch looking out over the sunlit valley. He was content to stand in the sunlight which slanted under the porch; he rested against the thick ivy which hid the wall. The place was sheltered and the wind which blew from the moor, sharp and biting and intensified near the angles of the new buildings, was imperceptible here.

Habit had altered him. He was well used to the fact that events which had seemed to be of imminent importance were now lost to memory, while other occurrences, borne of chance and trivial enough at the time of their happening, had taken on a direct significance which had modified his way of life and even his way of thinking. He was a man more observant of changes within himself than of changes in his surroundings; at the same time he was no longer surprised by the changes which had taken place. He no longer had a keen sense of enquiry. A few years ago he believed that the accidence of the letter and his attitude to its initial arrival had begun the alteration within himself; now he was inclined to think that these two things had merely been symptomatic of change. All that apart, he knew that the very events which had resulted in, or had been symptomatic of, that arbitrary but undercutting alteration had become the support by which he now lived. Change, arbitrary change, had become mundane.

How much of the alteration within himself had been of his own making? How much had been the unforeseen result of muddled reaction to the changes within his circumstances?

He was interrupted in his thoughts by the sound of someone walking up the drive. He leaned forward; he shared the universal interest in the arrival of any newcomer.

There was a brisk determination about the man who walked up the drive. He looked about, taking in the new buildings with a glance and dismissing them almost as if he had expected to see them there. For some reason Alexander found his cursory glance disturbing; the new buildings, angular and colourlessly grey, continued to surprise him every time he looked at them. Perhaps the newcomer saw them as only one part of a new landscape and accepted them as being buildings which he might have expected to see.

170

The newcomer, in dismissing his surroundings, evinced a self-assurance which bordered on the arrogant. He stood in front of the door, removing his gloves. He took a letter from his pocket.

'This is the house?'

Alexander glanced at the half-unfolded paper which the newcomer held out to him and looked away. 'This is number twenty-eight,' he said.

'Then I am correct.'

The air was still and warm. Deep within the building, beyond the closed door, a telephone rang; it continued to ring for some time and then stopped unexpectedly as though the caller's patience had become exhausted. Down in the town a whistle sounded from the station and a train drew away.

'How do I get in?' The newcomer had been examining the ivy; his question had been an involuntary exclamation of exasperation, not addressed to Alexander. He had found the bell-pull. The interior bell rang distantly.

Alexander withdrew from asking the obvious questions even of himself. Who was this man? What was the nature of his appointment? What was the nature of the letter he had held out as though for examination? Alexander had asked those questions long ago: what was the purpose in asking them of a stranger? He left the porch and began to walk down the drive, unobtrusively, keeping to the verge where the grass was shaded by the high laurel hedge. Behind him he heard the sound of the door opening; he made an effort to avoid overhearing the conversation which had begun; he had no wish to listen to the dialogue of two people who could not understand each other.

When Alexander had reached the lodge gates he looked briefly back. The door of the house was open, but the servant who had opened it had returned inside. The traveller stood looking in, silently waiting for the invitation to enter. His assurance seemed to foretell a loneliness which for the moment he was unable to perceive.

*   *   *

What, at the end of it all, caused Alexander to leave the house? The arrival of the newcomer had nothing to do with it, even though there had been a sense of something seen before in the way in which he had unfolded his letter, as though for universal inspection, as if it were a thing which had the authority of a universal passport.

The glance he had taken at that letter, half unfolded and unread as it was, made Alexander recall something of his own circumstances. He remembered his last meeting with Mr Tompkins when his own letter had been discussed.

'I am always there at the crisis,' Mr Tompkins had said. 'You have always taken the pessimistic option. Where there has been doubt you have always looked on the possibilities with a dark view. Long ago, when you received a letter, you saw in it a summons, an indiction, a condemnation, even though the letter still remained open for your interpretation. The original letter had an open neutrality: the facsimile you made was an enclosed and an inward-looking copy of the original. Each sentence was qualified by doubt. What made you read the future like that?'

When Alexander left the house he mistook the premonition of illness for a natural tiredness. He had walked through the town and had reached the further edge of the park; his short journey had taken him longer than he had anticipated; ahead of him the footbridge crossed the river with a single high-arched span.

The bridge was an unnecessarily high iron structure with broad hand-rails and balusters of iron, each cast in a repetitive pattern of stiff leaves, indistinct under the layers of green paint. He found the ascent of the bridge difficult; in his weakness he was forced to grasp the hand-rail and to rely on it to keep his balance. His slow progress and the sound of his own heavy footfalls made him angry: his anger was increased because he knew that as a boy he would have leapt up the bridge, delighting to hear the stamp of his footsteps on the hollow iron pavement.

When he had reached the summit of the bridge he leaned on one of the hand-rails and looked down at the river. His face and body were wet with the sweat of his exertion. With incongruous hindsight he recalled the motto of his distant university, as though the three words had taken on an apt salience: 'preparation is wisdom'. The motto had been engraved above many an arch in the stiff script of the last century; unlike similar institutions of similar age his university had not latin-ized the legend. But, with the sight of the open country ahead of him, the recollection was unimportant.

Beyond the bridge the land was marshy and sectioned by ditches, now almost full of water which, still and dark, was speckled with fallen leaves. The branches of the unpollarded willow trees vaulted up into the sky. The wind, imperceptible as it had been to him while he walked, was noisy in the foliage.

He saw a man digging a grave. 'An unusual place,' he thought. 'Perhaps they bury them where they fall.'

It took him some time to reach the gravedigger for he had to cross the plank bridge which spanned a wide ditch. His balance was imperfect and he knew that if he fell he would find it difficult to rise again. When he stood in the same field as the gravedigger he was forced to wait to regain his breath, and when he resumed his progress he found the tall stems of the grasses to be an impediment. He reached the grave and sat, exhausted, on the bole of a fallen willow tree; the tree must have fallen recently for its leaves were still alive and the long rent in the heart-wood of its trunk was still white.

He was unwilling to look at the grave and he turned his head towards the hill behind him. Neither the house nor the new buildings were visible in the space left by the fallen tree; he could see only the rising moorland of the hill and the distant crags which gave him the impres-sion that he had travelled much further than he had.

The gravedigger climbed out of the hole. Alexander

had thought that he recognized him while he had stood afar; now he was not so certain. The gravedigger was not a man from the house, he was certain of that, but at the same time it was difficult to say where he had come from or who had instructed him to dig this solitary grave here. The gravedigger rested on the iron bar he had been using to lever rocks and looked out across the river, his attention resting on something which momentarily interested him.

'It's an unusual place for a grave,' said Alexander.

The gravedigger looked down at him. 'It is. It's too near the river. This land is all watermeadow; it will be flooded for four months of the year.' He said these things as though they were generalities; perhaps he wished to distance himself from Alexander. 'I must get on with it or it will fill with water.'

Alexander stirred at the cogency of the remark. He stood, cautiously, for he was very weak; when he tried to stand he heard his own pulse in his head. He struggled against a weakness he had never experienced before; a roaring sound filled his ears and for a moment he was unable to see.

He had fallen at the lip of the grave; his sight returned and he looked downward at the bottom of the hole where the water was beginning to collect. The fact that his senses had failed, even momentarily, had made him very afraid; how would he perceive things in the future without them?' 'How long will it be before he arrives?' He spoke with difficulty; he found that he could no longer raise his head.

The gravedigger, with a sudden compassion for Alexander and seeing the extremity of his illness, straddled the grave and reached out his hands to support him. He had misheard the question. 'Not long, to look at you,' he said. He lifted Alexander, pulling him so that he leaned against the fallen willow trunk. He put an enamel jug of beer into Alexander's hand, but, finding that he made no effort to grasp it, he placed the rim to his lips. When he saw that no beer was swallowed he put the jug down on the ground.

174

'What is the procedure when he comes? I do not want to remain a servant for ever.' Alexander had spoken surprisingly loudly. 'Nevertheless, I must know the procedure and follow it.'

The gravedigger held Alexander's head in his hands; without this support Alexander would certainly have fallen on his side. It was clear that he had not heard what Alexander had said.

Unable to turn his head, Alexander looked up into the gravedigger's eyes as though through them he might perceive the immediacy of coming events. 'What is his real name?' This was the question which he had intended to ask; his face was set, for a moment, in an expression of enquiry, though this expression may have been caused by the way in which the gravedigger supported his head. The question was not asked, though, for it had been forgotten at the instant of its formulation.

THE END